'So why hav[e]

'Once was enou[gh]
'Besides, I'm to[o]
want to take me on at my age...too set in my ways.'

'Rubbish! You're a very attractive woman.' Matthew's eyes travelled the length of her slender body and she reacted almost as though he had touched her, tightening her fingers around the stem of her glass to control their tremor.

Josie Metcalfe lives in Cornwall now with her long-suffering husband, four children and two horses, but, as an Army brat frequently on the move, books became the only friends who came with her wherever she went. Now that she writes them herself she is making new friends, and hates saying goodbye at the end of a book—but there are always more characters in her head clamouring for attention until she can't wait to tell their stories.

Recent titles by the same author:

LOUD AND CLEAR
FORGOTTEN PAIN
BOUND BY HONOUR
A VOICE IN THE DARK
SEEING EYE TO EYE
HELL ON WHEELS
SECRETS TO KEEP

WORTH WAITING FOR

BY
JOSIE METCALFE

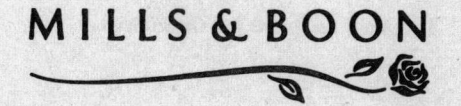

MILLS & BOON

DID YOU PURCHASE THIS BOOK WITHOUT A COVER?
If you did, you should be aware it is **stolen property** as it was reported *unsold and destroyed* by a retailer. Neither the Author nor the publisher has received any payment for this book.

All the characters in this book have no existence outside the imagination of the author, and have no relation whatsoever to anyone bearing the same name or names. They are not even distantly inspired by any individual known or unknown to the author, and all the incidents are pure invention.

All rights reserved including the right of reproduction in whole or in part in any form. This edition is published by arrangement with Harlequin Enterprises II B.V. The text of this publication or any part thereof may not be reproduced or transmitted in any form or by any means, electronic or mechanical, including photocopying, recording, storage in an information retrieval system, or otherwise, without the written permission of the publisher.

This book is sold subject to the condition that it shall not, by way of trade or otherwise, be lent, resold, hired out or otherwise circulated without the prior consent of the publisher in any form of binding or cover other than that in which it is published and without a similar condition including this condition being imposed on the subsequent purchaser.

MILLS & BOON, the Rose Device and
LOVE ON CALL are trademarks of the publisher.
Harlequin Mills & Boon Limited,
Eton House, 18-24 Paradise Road, Richmond, Surrey TW9 1SR

© Josie Metcalfe 1996

ISBN 0 263 79764 3

Set in Times 10 on 12 pt. by
Rowland Phototypesetting Limited
Bury St Edmunds, Suffolk

03-9608-45269

Made and printed in Great Britain

CHAPTER ONE

'I'M GETTING married!'

Hope's heart sank as she heard the voice, its tone a mixture of happiness and defiance. She'd only just come home from a gruelling shift at the hospital and she really wasn't ready to cope with this.

'When?' The headache she'd been fighting off took hold with a vengeance. 'Have you set a date?'

'Well, Edward and I were hoping for midsummer, but the hotel didn't have any vacancies then. . . But it will definitely be before September.'

'But you're not even halfway through your course. You've got so much to—'

'I've asked Liz and Anne to be bridesmaids and I've seen just the dress. . .' Predictably Jane's voice cut over the words she didn't want to hear, trying to bury them under an avalanche of details.

'Jane. . .' Hope toed off her shoes and sank wearily into the corner of the sofa closest to the telephone. 'Can you come home for the weekend so that we can talk about this?'

'I'm loaded down with essays at the moment.' She heard the defensive tone colouring the words. 'And anyway there's not much point in discussing it. Edward and I know what we're doing and it's up to us.'

For a moment Hope cursed the fact that she'd taken Jane to the reception at the hospital where she'd met Edward Benedict, then pulled a remorseful face. There was nothing wrong with the young man really; he was intelligent and hard-working and he seemed to care a great deal for Jane, but he was so...so immature and self-centred.

'We've chosen the hotel for the reception.' Jane's voice broke into her thoughts. 'You'll love it—the room we've booked is so beautiful.'

'Well...' Hope massaged her forehead, where the headache was thumping hardest. 'If you send me the information about it, I'll have a look. You sent for brochures from several, did you?'

'Oh, yes. Edward and I weeded through them and had a look at the better ones...' And chose the most expensive, Hope thought knowingly. It had been like that this last year, since the two of them had started going out together.

'Have you got details you could send me?'

'Oh, there's no need for that. We've already booked it provisionally. All they need is a cheque for the deposit.' She airily mentioned an amount that hit Hope with a sickening thud. Surely Jane realised how difficult it would be to find that sort of sum on a nurse's wages—and that was only the deposit.

'I'd still like to see the brochure,' she insisted quietly, feeling as if her head would explode if she raised her voice any higher. 'You know how tight money is at the moment, and I had actually hoped that I would be giving you your reception myself...' Her skill in the kitchen had almost persuaded her to take it up as a career instead of nursing when Jon had...

'This is *my* wedding.' The voice on the other end of the phone rose stridently. '*You* might have been happy with second best all your life, but it's not what *we* want.'

Hope was left holding the buzzing receiver as her daughter slammed the phone down on her.

'Oh, damn.' She dropped her head back wearily against the sofa and dragged the fingers of both hands through the bedraggled waves of her short dark blonde hair. She'd known she was too tired to cope with the bombshell as soon as it had landed in her lap, but she'd had no idea she'd make such a mess of it.

'Oh, Jane,' she sighed. 'Where did I go wrong?' She closed her eyes tight, willing the helpless tears away. If only there was someone to talk to when she didn't know what to do, someone to help shoulder the burden of bringing up a daughter single-handedly.

She laughed wryly. How many times had she wished the same thing in the years since they'd lost Jon? It had never made any difference before, so why should it now?

She struggled out of the soft upholstery and stood up, straightening to her full five feet three.

'If wishes were horses then beggars would ride,' she muttered as she grabbed the discarded shoes and shuffled through to her tiny bedroom. She was too tired tonight to start thinking about the nightmare the next few months would be. She knew Jane well enough to predict that every step of the arrangements would be turned into a bloody battle as she tried to drag her daughter's feet back down to the ground.

It hadn't always been like that... A wan smile crossed her face briefly as she remembered the sunny, generous nature with which her little girl had been blessed.

It was the last year which had changed all that—ever since she had started to mix with Edward's crowd. It wasn't that they were Hooray Henrys—none of them had enough money to spend all day in frivolity and they all had to earn their livings—but they all seemed to have the same selfish attitude that it was their right to have whatever they wanted and it was their parents' duty to provide the money for it.

The worst part of the whole situation was the fact that Edward Benedict was the nephew and ward of Matthew Benedict, who just happened to be the paediatric consultant at St Augustine's and hence her boss.

Life had been so much simpler a year ago.

Jane had done well in her final school exams and had found a holiday job on the auxiliary staff at the hospital while she waited to start her university course. It was the end of an era, and Hope had viewed it with mixed feelings.

There was, of course, a sense of pride at her daughter's achievements, but there was also a strange feeling of regret for the loss of her child.

Once, she had hoped that she would have several children, but it was not to be. Now, at thirty-seven, she had regretfully resigned herself to the fact that the only children she would hold would be her patients at the hospital or her eventual grandchildren.

Her post as sister on the paediatric ward meant that she had been one of the first to be invited to the reception to welcome the new paediatric consultant to the staff.

'Are you going to buy a new dress?' Maggie demanded when she saw the formal invitation.

'Good Lord, no!' Hope's reaction was automatic. 'I've better things to spend my hard-earned wages on than a dress I'll never wear again. Besides, I can never find anything to fit me except kiddies' clothes, and they're hardly the right style for someone of my age.'

'Rhubarb!' Maggie retorted rudely. 'I'm older than you are.'

'And you were endowed with a grown-up's body!' Hope glanced pointedly from her own slenderness to the Staff Nurse's more generous figure.

'Shame we can't share it out between us, then there'd be two happy people,' Maggie laughed.

The topic was dropped for the time being but Hope knew that her friend would return to it sooner or later.

She huffed out a frustrated breath. There was never enough money to do all the things she would like. Sometimes it felt as though she'd been stretching pennies to do the work of pounds all her life.

At least the worst of it was over. Jane had finished school and would be receiving a grant for her university course in the autumn.

Hope had managed to scrape together the money to buy her an elderly Mini as soon as she had passed her test, and she was hoping that her daughter would be able to drive home to visit at intervals so that they could maintain their relationship.

She had an awful feeling that she might be very lonely without the presence of her bubbly daughter to fill the silent spaces in their little house.

Still, without the drain on her finances of driving lessons and extra tuition to help her achieve the grades she'd needed, perhaps she'd be able to travel up to visit Jane. It was so long since she'd had a holiday or bought herself something new just because she wanted it.

Despite her determination that she was going to wear her faithful basic black dress to the reception, she couldn't resist having a quick glance through the shelves in the corner of her room which housed her sewing materials.

'I'm certain I put a length of green...' she muttered as she sifted through the pile of unfinished projects. 'Oh, dear.' She held up a half-finished patchwork quilt. 'One of these days...' She tucked it back between some fur-fabric she'd bought to make soft toys for raffle prizes and the remnants from the curtains she'd made for Jane's room when they'd redecorated.

'Oh, yes...' She slid out a tissue-wrapped bundle and unfolded it to reveal the imported Thai silk she'd bought in a sale soon after she'd been appointed. She'd forgotten just how rich the colour was—a perfect mixture of emerald and deep forest-green with the two colours of threads running across each other.

It took several evenings, but years of make do and mend had made her skilled with her needle. By the time the evening of the reception arrived she was the proud possessor of a perfectly fitted pure silk cocktail dress that had cost her next to nothing to make.

'And this is Sister Morgan,' the unctuous voice of the hospital's chief administrator intoned as Hope held out her hand in turn. 'As you know, Mr Benedict is our new paediatric consultant...'

The hand which grasped hers was slim and long-fingered, but there was an underlying strength which surprised her almost as much as the warmth which drew her eyes upward towards his face.

Chilly grey-green eyes regarded her impassively

from a face which owed its shape and colouring to genes other than Anglo-Saxon. His hair was thick as thatch, and so blond that the sprinkling of grey at the temples was hardly evident. His eyebrows and lashes were several shades darker and gave definition to eyes as secretive as the depths of a mountain lake.

'Sister.' The deep voice was cool, and the single raised eyebrow drew her attention to the fact that she was still holding his hand while she catalogued his features.

'Oh.' She withdrew her fingers hurriedly, feeling the heat growing in her cheeks as she grasped the errant fingers with her other hand. 'Welcome to St Augustine's,' she murmured, and took a half-step backwards to allow the reception line to progress.

'Doubtless we'll have a chance to become better acquainted once we're working together.' His voice held a new husky tone which brought all Hope's antennae to belated attention, and she found herself betraying her nervousness as she twisted her narrow gold wedding ring around on her slender finger.

'Of course, sir,' she said, her calm voice hiding her agitation under a thin layer of frost.

For several seconds he stood silently in front of her and she could sense his confusion at her withdrawal, could almost feel him willing her to look at him, but she didn't allow her eyes to lift above the muted stripes of his pristine silk tie. Then, to her relief, he followed the promptings of the chief administrator and moved on.

Hope drew in a shaky breath and looked around the room for Jane. The invitation to this evening's reception had included a provision for her to invite a guest, and Jane had grudgingly agreed to accompany her.

'I'll be the only one there not in the queue for a Zimmer frame,' she'd grumbled teasingly, only changing her mind when she saw the effort Hope had made with her new dress.

Familiar laughter drew Hope's eyes across the room and she caught sight of her daughter's long ash-blond hair being tossed flirtatiously over one shoulder as she smiled up at the young man boxing her into the corner by the buffet. Trust Jane to find the best looking young man in the room and captivate him within minutes.

Hope accepted a glass of orange juice from the laden tray which appeared in front of her and sipped, relishing the cool liquid sliding down her throat as she tried to analyse her reaction to the department's new head.

Her eyes drifted across the room of their own accord to zero in on another head of blond hair, this one closely clipped against the curve of a male skull so that it left the strong column of a tanned neck open to her gaze. He really was a very good-looking man. . .

'Gorgeous, isn't he?' Maggie's irreverent giggle announced her arrival at Hope's elbow. 'He can take my temperature any day.'

'He's a paediatrician.' Hope tried to sound serious. 'That means he specialises in treating children, not grown women who behave like children.'

'Believe me—' Maggie's eyebrows wagged up and down lasciviously '—I don't want him to treat me like a child!'

'Maggie!' Hope was beginning to lose control of the urge to laugh at her colleague's nonsense.

'What?' Her friend's face was the picture of innocence. 'You can't tell me you haven't noticed that he's the best looking man we've ever had in the department? I know you don't date much but you must remember what hormones are for—you only have to look at him!'

Maggie's teasing comment carried clearly in the sudden lull, and Hope felt her cheeks blaze as she watched his blond head turn and his grey-green eyes pierced her like icicles.

Hope didn't sleep much that night, dreading going in to work the next day and having to face him after the embarrassment of the previous evening.

There had been no way during the excruciating remainder of the evening to explain that Maggie was a terrible tease and that her remarks had been a joke—Hope had hardly been able to bring herself to look at the man, let alone approach him and start an apology.

Luckily, Jane hadn't noticed how preoccupied she was, chattering all the way home about her latest conquest, her monologue peppered with 'Edward says. . .'

All Hope could remember as she dragged her tired body under the shower the next morning was that the young man her daughter had captivated yesterday evening shared the same surname as her nemesis and that within an hour she would be coming face to face with him.

After all her worry, her arrival on the ward was an anticlimax, coinciding with the bustle of an admission sent up from Casualty.

'Susan Allardyce, aged three.' Hope checked the details on the case-notes. 'Vomiting and abdominal pain. Query gastrointestinal bleeding due to iron poisoning.'

'Do we know the source and the maximum amount ingested?' Hope's pulse went into overdrive as she recognised the voice asking the question but she couldn't allow it to affect her concentration—a little girl's life might depend on it.

'Prenatal iron tablets. The prescription's been checked and the formulary lists the preparation she took as one of the higher concentrations. From the date of the prescription it looks as if she's taken close to a maximum dose for her size and age.'

'How far did they get downstairs?' Out of the corner of her eye Hope could see his blond head leaning towards their distressed patient as he checked her over.

'Blood has gone up for the serum iron level to be measured. They'll also be checking electrolytes and haemoglobin—'

'Group and cross-match?' the deep voice broke in succinctly.

'Done automatically when they're this vulnerable,' Hope confirmed, then continued, 'She was given intramuscular desferrioxamine to slow down her absorption of the iron and her stomach was washed out with a one per cent sodium bicarbonate solution with added desferrioxamine.'

'How long before we get the serum iron level results?' He looked up from his examination as Hope reached for her fob watch, and the sudden contact with his cool grey-green eyes stopped the breath in her throat for timeless seconds as she relived the shiver which his icy disdain had caused last night.

'Th—they should be here any minute,' she croaked briefly before she managed to control her breathing.

'Good. The sooner we know the figures, the sooner we can decide on the appropriate regimen. We've got to balance it quickly or she could go into shock, and the less gastrointestinal damage she suffers, the less likely she is to have strictures form later on.'

The phone rang then. It was a message from the lab with the initial figures and a promise that written confirmation would follow shortly.

'Looks like she was lucky this time.' The deep voice echoed the relief that spread through the team. 'Are the parents here?'

'One of my nurses took the mother through to my office.' Hope stepped back hurriedly to allow him to walk past her. 'She's nearly full-term with her second child.'

'You'd better come with me while I tell her what's been going on, then.' He threw the words back at her as he shouldered his way out through the door.

'Get her settled in the free bed in the side unit,' Hope directed her team as she stripped off her disposable gloves and apron. 'I'll bring her mum to her when he's spoken to her.' She nodded towards the tall figure quickly disappearing from view and sped after him.

'Mrs Allardyce? I'm Mr Benedict.' Hope closed the door behind the departing nurse as the paediatrician introduced himself to the heavily pregnant woman. There was a half-empty coffee-cup abandoned on the corner of her desk and a man-sized handkerchief was being twisted convulsively between white-knuckled fingers.

'Is Suzie. . .? Is she. . .dead?' She whispered through bloodless lips. 'It's all my fault. I should have locked them up in the bathroom, but I kept forgetting to take them. . .' Her words disintegrated into sobs.

'Mrs Allardyce. . .'

'No!' Before the paediatrician could say any more,

Hope was across the room and had her arm around the young woman's shoulders. 'She's not dead.'

'Not. . .?' Her tear-drenched eyes flicked from the warm blue-grey of Hope's to the cool grey-green of the consultant's steady gaze.

'We'll need to keep her in hospital under observation for at least thirty-six hours, but it looks as if she's been lucky,' his deep voice reassured her. 'We'll be testing her to see what long-term effects it might have on her, but it looks as if your quick reactions got her here in time to minimise them.'

'Can I. . .? When can I see her?'

Grey-green met blue-grey in an unspoken question.

'We'll have her settled in her bed in about five minutes,' Hope explained with a smile. 'I'll send the nurse along with a fresh cup of coffee while you're waiting and I'll let you know as soon as we're ready for you.'

'Is there somewhere I could phone for my husband?' Her hands were twisting the handkerchief again. 'He'll be finishing his shift soon and if he goes home and we're not there. . .'

'No problem.' Hope squeezed her chilly hands. 'If you let him know where Suzie's favourite toys are, he could bring them in with him——' As she spoke gently to calm the young woman down she was aware of movement out of the corner of her eye.

'If you've got any further questions?' The deep voice interrupted politely.

'No, Doctor.' A smile trembled on her lips as the woman struggled to get up. 'Thank you so much.'

'Just make certain that you find a safer place for your medicines before you've got two of them to get into mischief.' He nodded at her swollen belly and smiled briefly before leaving her to Hope's care.

That had been a year ago and in all that time there had been no mention between the two of them of the first time they'd met.

For a year she and Matthew Benedict had worked together in the close confines of the paediatric department, and the closest they had got to having an intimate conversation was a comment on the weather.

That didn't mean that they didn't work well together, they did—their reactions to their young charges equally dedicated and totally professional.

Hope sometimes wondered if she'd imagined the spark of awareness which had seemed to burn between them at their first meeting, the heat which had engulfed her fingers when he'd shaken her hand, the shiver of awareness which had made her nervously twist her wedding ring as his keen eyes had pierced her reserve.

That was all in the past.

Since her daughter's phone call everything had changed. In just a few short months Sister Hope Morgan would be related to Consultant Paediatrician Matthew Benedict by the marriage of her daughter to his nephew.

Hope shook her head as she was overwhelmed by a feeling of helplessness. It had happened so fast. One minute she was tentatively looking forward to an easing of the pressure which had fallen on her shoulders with Jane's flight from the nest, and the next she was being engulfed by a tidal-wave of acid-tongued recrimination.

She sighed dejectedly as she checked her heavy-eyed

appearance in the mirror over the basin the next morning, the dark circles under her eyes all too visible through the fine pale skin.

At some stage during the day she was going to have to find some way of speaking to Matthew without other ears overhearing the conversation. The last thing she wanted was for her personal problems to become grist for the hospital gossip mill.

All day it seemed as if everything was conspiring against her as he was paged backwards and forwards between the ward, Casualty and Theatre, so that it was the end of her shift before she finally saw her chance to speak to him without an audience.

'Mr Benedict?'

'Yes, Sister?' He paused on his way towards the doors to the unit and waited for her to catch him up, her arms laden with shopping bags and odds and ends.

'Can I. . .?' She bit her lip and started again. 'Have you got a moment free? I think it would be a good idea if we. . .spoke. . .?'

'Ah!' The frown which had been pleating his forehead disappeared. 'I take it you've seen your daughter?'

'No.' It was Hope's turn to frown. 'I haven't seen her for several weeks.'

'That's strange.' He seemed taken aback. 'Edward brought her over to see me at the weekend. . . Does that mean they haven't told you about their plans?'

The pain of her daughter's thoughtless betrayal was as sharp as a physical injury, and she felt herself sway with the impact.

'Jane came to see you. . .?' Her voice sounded strangely rusty. Her daughter had made a special journey to announce her plans to Edward's uncle, but her *mother* only warranted a phone call and a high-handed demand for a cheque.

'Of course.' He smiled. 'They made a point of coming over to make the announcement.'

'H-how nice.' She swallowed the bile which rose in her throat and tried to pin a smile to a face which didn't seem to want to obey her.

'Sister... Hope? Are you feeling all right?' He took hold of her elbow and gave it a little shake. 'You've gone quite pale. Is something wrong?'

'Wrong?' Hope tried to laugh, but her voice cracked with the effort. 'Of course not.' She tried to pull her arm out of his grasp, desperate to get away before the tears pressing behind her eyes fell in a scalding flood, but he tightened his grip. 'Please,' she whispered on a shuddering breath. 'I need to go h-home...'

She knew the instant he realised that something was seriously wrong, his eyes taking on their familiar coolly analytical gaze.

'Did you drive in this morning?' he demanded crisply, relieving her of her burden with one hand before turning towards the main exit and drawing her helplessly in his wake with a firm grasp on her elbow.

'Yes...no. My car's in for servicing...'

'Right. I'll drive you home.'

'No.' Hope tried to pull away. 'I can manage perfectly well.'

'I'm sure you can,' he agreed calmly without slowing his pace—without even looking towards her. 'But in this case there's no need.'

'But—'

'For goodness' sake, woman.' His exasperation showed even though he hadn't raised his voice. '*You* said you wanted to speak to me, but now I'm providing the means for you to do it you're fighting me every step of the way. Make up your mind.'

They'd come to a halt beside a dark green Jaguar saloon just as a flicker of lightning behind the bulk of the paediatric wing caught Hope's eye.

She drew in a breath to speak and heard a distant rumble.

'Thunder.' She pulled a face as she glanced towards the ominously piled clouds spilling over the horizon and a second rumble followed the first.

'That one wasn't.' The deep chuckle surprised her. 'That was my stomach.'

'When did you last feed it?' Hope grasped eagerly at the lighter atmosphere.

'I was trying to eat when you bleeped me for little Darren.' He referred to their newest patient, a three-year-old stroke victim, as he leant forward to open the passenger door.

'You haven't had anything since then?' Hope slid into the cushioned comfort and relaxed with a sigh, completely forgetting that she had been going to insist on getting home under her own steam. She settled her bags in the space beside her feet, then ran her fingers over the glove-soft leather. This was sheer luxury.

'Have you?' he countered as he stretched his long legs towards the pedals and turned the key in the ignition.

Hope was silent for a second as she appreciated the quiet skill of his driving then shook her head, realising that she still hadn't answered his question.

'I think that was the last time I ate too—apart from raiding the biscuit tin.'

'*That's* why there weren't any left when I went on the scrounge!' he teased, and Hope saw his solemn face crease with humour.

'I've got some more at home,' she heard herself offer, and could have bitten her tongue.

'If that offer comes with a cup of tea, I accept with alacrity,' he said, just before the weather delivered a vicious crack of lightning followed almost immediately by an earth-shattering roll of thunder.

Before the echoes had time to die away the heavens opened and rain fell in a deluge.

'Well. . .' He slowed the car and she could see that the wipers were having trouble keeping up with the volume of water lashing down at them. 'I hope you're properly grateful for my generous offer of a lift—or would you rather be out in this?'

Hope avoided commenting by giving him the next set of directions, which brought them to her front door.

'Are you sure you want to risk a soaking?' Hope released her seat belt and leant forward to gather up her bags. 'We could always put this off until—'

'Oh, no, you don't.' He switched off the engine and opened his door. 'You promised me a cup of tea and I'm going to hold you to it.'

Hope fumbled for her door key, holding it tightly in one hand as he swung the passenger door open, then making a dash for her front step.

Her breathing was ragged and her heart was beating far too fast as she reached for the light switch in the dimness of the hallway and continued through to the kitchen, but she knew that she was only trying to fool herself as she pretended it was the exertion of carrying a few bags of shopping which was causing it.

She lifted the lid of the kettle to check the level of water in it and set it to heat, horribly conscious of the sounds of her front door closing and the steady progress of footsteps coming towards her.

Hope bit her lip, hoping that the sharp pain would help her to bring herself under control. For heaven's sake, she had been working with the man for a year without any problem. Why should she be suddenly struck by a stupid juvenile awareness that he was in the same room as she was...?

'Any chance of a towel?'

Hope gasped and whirled towards the voice—and nearly collided with him. She hadn't realised that he was so close—almost close enough to lay her head on his shoulder, and definitely close enough to detect the lingering tang of the soap he used.

'Pardon?' Hope blinked and looked up at him, the early dusk brought on by the storm making her peer at him in the gloom.

'A towel?' he repeated patiently, and she saw a drop of water make its way from the rain-darkened strand of hair which lay across his forehead and run down the length of his nose.

'Oh, I'm sorry, sir... Of course...' She turned towards the drawers beside the sink and was flustered enough to open the wrong one first, staring in bemusement at the serried ranks of cutlery.

'Hope?' His calm voice was coloured with humour. 'I want to dry my head, not cut it off...'

'Oh!' The heat rushed up her throat and into her face as she shoved the drawer closed and retrieved a hand towel from the right one, turning reluctantly to hand it to him. 'I'm sorry, Mr Benedict—'

'Matthew,' he interrupted quietly, 'or Matt. After all, we're going to be related in a matter of weeks, so it seems a little silly for us to stand on ceremony...'

'Oh, God...' The memory of that awful phone call from Jane washed over her, reinforced by the new knowledge that Hope hadn't even been deemed worthy of a personal visit to break the news.

As quickly as that, Hope's feet returned to earth with a thud.

What on earth had she been doing, allowing herself to float off into some airy-fairy land of physical awareness with the man dripping all over her kitchen floor? Since that first handshake a year ago there hadn't been so much as the quiver of an eyelash to suggest that there was an attraction between the two of them.

Face it, Hope reminded herself sternly, his presence was not the prelude to a relationship; the impending marriage of her daughter to this man's nephew was the *only* reason why he was here in her house.

CHAPTER TWO

THE kettle began to hiss and Hope reached automatically for the tea-caddy and teapot. Her thoughts were concentrated on the disturbing presence of Matthew Benedict leaning casually in the doorway behind her, and only long years of practice had her going through the motions of assembling the necessary items on a tray without needing to think about it.

'Would you like to come through to the sitting room?' she said as she turned towards the door, her eyes fixed firmly on the tell-tale ripples on the surface of the milk.

'May I carry the tray for you?' Two hands appeared in her field of vision.

'No! Thank you,' she tacked the polite words on the end of her blunt refusal, not daring to look up at him. She needed something to hang onto, something ordinary to occupy her hands and brain until she could get rid of him. . .until she could lick her wounds in private like an injured animal. . .

'Do you take milk——?' she began, but her throat closed up as she realised how farcical the whole situation was, and the jug landed with a crash among the elegant china.

'Hope!' He was there, taking her hands in his and turning them this way and that. 'Are you all right? Did you burn yourself?'

'Yes. . . I mean, no. . . Oh, God, I don't know *what*

I mean...' And to her horror she burst into tears.

'Hey!' A strong arm circled her shoulders supportively and she was guided back into the corner of the settee. 'It can't be as bad as all that, whatever it is,' he teased as he offered a neatly folded handkerchief.

'Can't it?' Hope sobbed as she shook out the pristine white fabric and buried her face in the cool softness. 'How would you know?'

For long seconds the room was silent but for the sound of Hope's stifled sobs.

'Tell me.' The words were spoken softly, encouragingly. 'Is it the sudden realisation that your little girl is all grown up?'

'Is she?' Hope couldn't help the touch of acid in her tone. 'I would have thought consideration for other people's feelings was more a mark of maturity than a sudden selfish decision to get married.'

'That's one way of looking at it, I suppose.' His cool tone made her scrub the tears from her cheeks so that she could face him with some dignity left intact, but he continued speaking almost immediately. 'You don't think that your reaction might be caused by a touch of jealousy?'

'You think I'm jealous?' Shock at his accusation almost robbed her of speech. 'Of my daughter?'

'Well, she is a very pretty young lady, just starting out on one of life's adventures. It wouldn't be unreasonable to suppose that her mother would see that as evidence that she was no longer of primary importance in her daughter's life any more.'

'No,' Hope agreed wryly. 'Just my chequebook.'

'That's something I think we need to sort out between us right from the start.' He seemed glad that she had mentioned the topic herself. 'Weddings are an expensive item, and I think it's only fair that the cost should be shared. It doesn't make sense that you should be saddled with the burden when I'm in a much better position to afford—'

'No,' Hope broke in, stung by his easy assumption. 'I always promised Jane that when she got married I would make her wedding dress for her and provide the cake.' She drew her breath in with a hiccup. 'I wanted to give her the perfect wedding, but if they've decided that they'd rather have expensive ostentation. . .' She shrugged.

'There's no reason why they shouldn't have the perfect wedding. Between the two of us, we can easily afford whatever they want.'

'And throwing money at it will make it perfect?' Hope challenged. 'What about the marriage itself? What meaning is there in that? They hardly know each other and they decide out of the blue that they're going to have a big, splashy wedding in a swanky hotel.' She shook her head despairingly. 'From what I've seen over the years, the more money there is spent on a wedding, the faster the couple end up getting divorced.'

'That's very cynical.' His voice was thoughtful, and she saw that his eyes were fixed on her hands as she twisted her wedding ring around with betraying fingers. 'Was that what happened with your own marriage?'

For several seconds his question robbed her of breath, as though he'd winded her with an unexpected blow.

'You couldn't be further from the mark.' Hope's chin rose belligerently as she laced her fingers tightly together to keep them still. It took all her determination for her to meet his critical gaze without flinching.

'So why aren't you and your husband still together?' His question was abrasive.

'Because he's dead,' Hope said flatly.

For several seconds he didn't move, as though her words had shocked him. Finally he drew in a hesitant breath, but before he could speak the electric silence was filled by an insistent bleeping sound, and he reached for his pager with a muttered curse and pressed the button to silence it.

'I'm sorry,' he murmured, then paused, clearly in two minds about what to do first.

Hope knew that their conversation about the impending wedding was far from over, but, after working with him for the past year, she knew that the call of duty would be too strong to ignore.

'The telephone's on the table beside you,' she prompted as relief swept over her. Briefly, as she watched his lean fingers tap out the familiar number, she felt guilty for her selfish reaction. She knew that he would only have been paged if one of his charges needed his specialised help, and she wondered which of them had suffered a set-back.

The conversation was brief. Within seconds he was putting down the handset and straightening up out of the soft upholstery. Hope stood too, recognising his need to go.

'I'll have to get back straight away. Admission to Paediatrics from a crash.'

He hesitated in the doorway, turning back to gaze at her with eyes that seemed more grey than green.

'Will you be all right?' For the first time since Hope had met him he sounded hesitant.

'Of course I will.' She straightened her shoulders and stood tall. 'I've been taking care of myself for a good many years now.'

He nodded, his forehead pleating briefly as he delved one hand in his pocket to retrieve his car keys.

'We'll have to talk again when we've had a chance to speak to Edward and Jane. There must be some simple way of sorting everything out.' His mouth twisted wryly and he raised one lean-fingered hand in a brief farewell before he disappeared into the hall and out of her front door.

'And the best of luck to you,' Hope muttered as she sank back into the corner of the settee, knowing that the situation was likely to get more complicated as time went on.

She thought back to the abrupt ending of her conversation with her daughter and the pain assailed her again. The tears brimmed in her eyes as the disillusionment flooded through her. Did Jane care so little for her that she would deliberately hurt her in this way?

As she blew her streaming nose she realised that she was still clutching a large white handkerchief, and through her tears she saw the burgundy curlicues of an embroidered 'M' in one corner.

'Monogrammed handkerchiefs,' she sobbed in disgusted disbelief. 'No wonder his nephew wants a pretentious wedding.' And she curled up in the corner of the settee and buried her face in the squashed patchwork cushion that Matthew had been leaning against as she gave way to her misery.

When she finally went to bed Hope slept heavily, worn out by her tears. She woke with a dull headache which wasn't improved when she remembered that she didn't have a car to get to work.

'Still raining,' she muttered as she peered out of the window. 'I'll get soaked if I wait at the bus stop just as much as if I walk to the hospital. . .' She sighed heavily as she reached for the telephone directory and riffled through until she found the listing for taxis.

Within a couple of minutes she had arranged her transport and was sitting in the chair by the window. From there she had an uninterrupted view of the road, so that she would be able to see the taxi arrive, but instead of congratulating herself on a sensible decision she found herself feeling guilty about the expense.

'Too many years of stretching every penny,' she admitted ruefully to the empty room, then gave herself a shake. 'I'm the one earning the money so I darn well deserve to spend enough of it on myself to make sure I don't get soaked on the way to work.'

She gathered up her belongings as she heard the sound of a vehicle slowing down.

'After all,' she rationalised under her breath as she let herself out of the front door, 'this trip is a damn sight more necessary than a swanky limousine to take me to a pretentious wedding.' And she pulled the door shut behind her with a sharp snap.

The short journey to the hospital was just long enough for Hope to stabilise her thoughts, and she paid the cabbie with a smile.

'Worth every penny,' she commented as she opened the door onto the latest downpour.

'Perhaps I should have charged you double,' he quipped as he flipped his sign ready to join his colleagues in the rank by the hospital entrance.

Hope laughed as she sped across the wet tarmac and the doors slid open for her.

'Who was the new one last night?' she asked Doris as soon as she reached the ward, her slender fingers flicking through the row of files.

'There were two of them—came in together.' Doris slid them out and passed them across. 'Sisters walking home from the swimming pool with their mother when a van ploughed into them.'

'Dear God!' Hope breathed in horror. 'Why?'

'Driver had a heart attack at the wheel and lost control. He was dead before the paramedics got to him. Hey!' Her colleague abandoned her usual calm to exclaim. 'How did you know we'd had some new ones? You'd already gone home.'

Hope bit her lip as colour rushed swiftly into her cheeks, and she silently cursed her unruly tongue.

'My car's in the garage and Mr Benedict gave me a lift home last night.' She cursed again as she saw the spark of interest in her colleague's eyes grow brighter. 'He used my phone to call in when his pager went off and came straight in to see the two girls.' She surreptitiously crossed her fingers in the hope that her specially edited version of events would satisfy Doris.

'But—'

'Sister...'

Hope breathed a sigh of relief at the interruption and plunged straight into the business of the day, making sure that there was no chance for any more questions before Doris went off duty.

Not that she had anything to hide, she argued silently to herself as she comforted a frightened five-year-old as he was prepared for an emergency appendicectomy.

There had been nothing illicit in the two of them being together last night, but their meeting concerned a private matter, something between his family and hers, and the longer it remained that way the better.

Hope was grateful that the morning was frantically busy—if she hadn't had so much to occupy her mind and hands, her next talk with Matthew Benedict would have been looming over her like the storm clouds last night.

This morning she was hard pushed to keep everything running smoothly in the ward, but she found herself welcoming the hectic pace.

'Maggie.' Hope beckoned the staff nurse over. 'There's been a bit of a delay in Theatre. Lisa's waiting to go down next to have her grommets in her ears, but her mother's beginning to get herself in a state.'

'I'll get her a drink and calm her down a bit.' Maggie smiled. 'The kiddie's definitely coping better than the parents, isn't she?'

'Perhaps we should give *them* pre-med, too. . .' Hope joked as she sped towards the telephone summons.

Several minutes later she was faced with a fresh challenge.

'Nurse, we've got another one transferring across to us from Intensive Care.' She grabbed the most experienced of her younger staff and primed her. 'They've got an emergency admission coming in with breathing difficulties and need the bed, so they're moving one of theirs out to us.'

Hope glanced down at her hasty notes. 'She's eleven and she's been with them for three weeks since she came over the handlebars of her bike.' She led the way towards the corner bed closest to the nurses' station.

'If you'll get this bed ready for her now, she should be with us in the next half-hour.'

'Do we know what injuries she has?' Polly Turner lost no time in asking.

'Head,' said Hope succinctly. 'Luckily there was no major damage to her neck, and the abnormalities initially showing on the brain scan have largely subsided.' She nodded her approval of the young woman's work and continued, 'She will have gradually been allowed to come off the sedative drugs once they were certain that her brain wasn't going to swell and cause permanent damage.'

'If it swells too far it can cause brain death, can't it?'

'Exactly,' Hope confirmed. 'She was very lucky. Apparently she hit a wall head-first. . .' She grimaced. 'Anyway, now they've got her stabilised enough to come off the monitors and she's ready to come onto a normal ward.'

The sound of the safety catches on the double doors into the ward being released drew their eyes across to the new arrival.

The slender figure of the young girl looked almost lost in the cage formed by the safety rails either side of her bed, the space beyond her feet piled high with her case-notes and equipment for the journey.

Hope's heart went out to her new charge as she watched the dark eyes slide blankly over the cheerful decoration of her latest abode.

'Hello, Stephanie.' Hope glanced quickly at the chart as she directed the positioning of the bed. 'I'm Sister Morgan.'

With a minimum of fuss the youngster was settled into the ward, just in time for her parents to arrive.

'Mr and Mrs Plews.' Hope welcomed them with a smile and grabbed an extra chair to set it beside their daughter's bed. 'I expect you're delighted with Stephanie's progress. She's doing really well.'

'We can't believe it.' Her mother reached for the pale hand lying on the covers, carefully avoiding the coils of intravenous tubes. 'When she first came in we didn't know if she was going to live, then we didn't know if she was going to be seriously brain-damaged. It's like a miracle to have her well enough to move out of Intensive Care to a normal ward. It seems to have happened so fast...'

Her eyes flicked to focus on something over Hope's shoulder just as she became aware that someone had come to stand behind her and turned to look.

'Mr Benedict.' Hope nodded in acknowledgement, fiercely squashing down the mixture of pleasure and apprehension she felt at seeing him there.

'Sister.' He was equally polite. 'Is everything all right here?'

'Fantastic.' Mr Plews beamed. 'My wife was just saying how quickly Stephanie's progressing. We were sat beside her for weeks, and suddenly...' He shook his head.

'The staff on Intensive Care will have told you that your daughter had to be kept unconscious so that they could control the swelling in her brain caused by her accident?' His deep voice was professionally soothing, but Hope could see how well her patient's parents were responding to it as they smiled and agreed.

'Once the scan showed that she was improving, and that the pressure had dropped inside her skull, they were able to lessen the drugs gradually and allow her to wake up.'

'We're just so grateful that she's going to be all right again,' her mother said in a quivery voice.

'She's still got a fair way to go,' Matthew warned. 'She'll need some concentrated physiotherapy to get her on her feet again because she's been in bed for so long, but with a bit of luck and a lot of hard work you'll soon have her home.'

'Sister?' There was a quiet urgency to Maggie's voice from the doorway of the side-ward. 'Can you ask Mr Benedict to have a look at Cheryl?'

'What's the problem?' Hope glanced back towards the Plews family but they were still talking to Matthew, so she made her way swiftly towards the worried staff nurse.

'She was doing very well after the accident, but she's not looking so good now. Her blood pressure's dropping as if she's losing blood. . .' She showed Hope the latest figures on the young girl's chart.

'You're right. It's a definite downward trend.' Hope handed it back as she cast her own professional eye over the pale features, noting how dark the bruising was becoming after Cheryl's contact with the runaway van. 'I'll get him in straight away to check her over. It looks as if she might have some internal damage which didn't show up when she was admitted.'

Hope's feet whispered swiftly over the gleaming floor as she made her way back towards the corner bed, and as she approached the adults grouped at its foot Matthew's head turned towards her, his grey-green eyes questioning under raised brows.

Her nod was enough to have him politely excusing

himself from a far more relaxed set of parents, and he joined her in the centre of the room.

'Problems?'

Hope nearly smiled at his unfailing directness, but concentrated on answering the question instead.

'It's the younger of the two girls involved with the van driver who had the heart attack—' she began.

'Cheryl?' he queried, and turned unerringly towards her room.

'Yes.' Once again, Hope was surprised when he remembered the name of his little charge. In the year since they'd been working together she'd never heard him get one wrong. 'Her blood pressure's dropping slowly but steadily. Do you think she might have some internal bleeding?'

'Almost certainly, dammit.' He pulled a face. 'I'll have a quick look at her now, but it might mean another trip to Theatre.'

Hope watched his long fingers examining the little body as gently as possible while his deep voice kept up a soothing commentary.

It wasn't many minutes before he caught her eye across the bed and gave a confirming nod.

'Poor kid,' he muttered as he reached for the phone in her office. 'It wasn't enough that she lost yards of skin and had her arm broken. Now it looks as if her spleen might have been damaged... Hello?' He ran the fingers of his free hand through the thickness of his straight blond hair and left it in spiky disarray as he waited to be connected with the duty anaesthetist.

Hope breathed a sigh of relief when Cheryl left the ward *en route* for Theatre almost immediately. She'd had extra blood run in through her IV to compensate for the amount she was losing, but there was no alternative to finding the cause of the bleeding and stopping it.

'Now all we've got to do is reorganise the rest of the ward routine,' she muttered as she studied the revised theatre times for her other patiently waiting charges.

The only good thing about the unexpectedly chaotic situation on the ward was that it left less time for her to think about the next talk she was due to have with a certain paediatrician.

The other advantage she'd recently discovered about her busy professional life was that when she was calming worried parents and supervising the care of post-operative children she couldn't concentrate on the sad fact that *her* daughter had made no attempt to speak to her since she'd slammed the phone down.

'Hope?'

The voice on the other end of the telephone addressed her by her first name, and it was several seconds before she realised who it was.

'Mr Benedict.' She couldn't help the surprised tone in her voice. He was the last person she had expected to hear on the other end when the phone had started ringing as soon as she got home. As she'd raced to answer it she'd actually been praying that her caller would be Jane. . .

'I thought we agreed you were going to call me Matt?' the deep velvety voice chided gently.

'I'm sorry.' She was glad that he couldn't see the warmth rising in her cheeks at the implied intimacy. 'Was there a problem on the ward after I left?'

'No. . .this isn't hospital business.' He sounded strangely diffident. 'I thought it would be a good idea if we met up for that talk. We didn't have time to sort anything out last time.'

Hope drew in a silent breath as her heart performed a totally unnecessary somersault, and wondered at the cause.

'What do you suggest?' She hoped that her voice didn't sound nearly as breathless to him as it did to her own ears. 'We might be able to snatch some time tomorrow if we both take our lunchbreak—'

'What about this evening?' he broke in. 'You haven't been home long enough to have eaten yet, have you? If I come for you at seven?'

'You want to take me out?' Hope could have bitten her tongue off when she heard the blatant incredulity in her words. What on earth was happening to her?

'Well, we both have to eat, and we need to talk, so it makes sense to combine the two...'

His tone was so matter-of-fact and his reasoning so eminently logical that Hope was still kicking herself when she put the phone down. She had still been fighting with her embarrassment, so that the rest of his words had floated over her head in a haze.

All she could remember was murmuring her agreement to be ready at seven while inside she was cringing at what he must be thinking. She must have sounded as eager as any desperately lonely widow at the chance of a good-looking man taking her out.

'But I'm not,' she said defiantly as she zipped herself into a favourite lightweight summer dress. 'I'm quite happy with my life just the way it is.' Her natural curls were given a brisk brushing until they crackled with energy, the paler blonde strands at the front gleaming in the light over her bathroom mirror as she leant forward to check that her make-up was smudge-free before she left the room.

The bell rang on the dot of seven, and she picked up her small evening bag on her way to the door.

She reached out her hand towards the catch and paused, drawing in a shaky breath and holding it for several seconds to calm herself, glad that the door was solid wood so that the man waiting outside couldn't see what she was doing.

'Good evening,' she said as she swung the door open.

He was caught with one hand raised to ring the bell again, and it stayed in mid-air while the two of them took each other's measure.

As she looked at him Hope had the strangest feeling that she hadn't really seen him before. It was like looking at a stranger as she took in the faultless tailoring of his dark suit and the crisp freshness of his white shirt against the golden tan of his skin.

This evening his eyes looked more green than grey, the planes of his cheeks more distinct, his jawline firmer as he appeared to clench his teeth.

'Hope.' He nodded, his expression serious, his gaze almost intimidating as he took in the picture she made.

Suddenly Hope realised that it was the first time he had seen her out of uniform since their first disastrous meeting, and she was glad that she had chosen a dress which matched her blue-grey eyes so well. The fact that she was looking her best gave her confidence the boost she needed to start the evening.

'I'm ready.' Hope indicated the bag in her hand. 'Or. . .did you want to come in for a drink first. . .?' She stepped backwards to invite him in, suddenly flustered because the situation had never occurred before and she didn't know what the correct etiquette was for such things.

'No.' One hand was raised to halt her retreat. 'We can go straight away. Perhaps you'll invite me in for coffee when I bring you back later.' And he stepped aside to allow her to lock the door before escorting her to the waiting car.

'I hope you don't mind, but I took the liberty of booking a table at the Thatched Cottage—unless you'd rather go somewhere else?' In no time he was deftly manoeuvring the car through the traffic in the centre of town as he took them towards the outskirts furthest away from the hospital. It was an area Hope hadn't had time to explore since she'd moved to St Augustine's, but had always promised herself that she would.

'No. That's fine. I've heard it's very good,' she said stiffly, uncomfortable with the unaccustomed need to make small talk.

'So, I've managed to choose somewhere you haven't been before.' He sounded pleased and the atmosphere lightened.

'That isn't difficult,' Hope chuckled. 'I haven't been to *any* of the local restaurants.'

'You prefer to go further afield for your social outings, do you?' He sounded almost intrigued.

'It's more a case of not going on social outings at all,' Hope admitted.

'Why on earth not? It can't be for lack of opportunity.'

'You're very gallant.' Hope focused her gaze out through the windscreen, glad that he was occupied with driving when she felt the heat of embarrassment scorch her cheekbones as she opted for honesty. 'But mostly it's financial. There hasn't been enough money for expensive outings while I've been bringing Jane up on a nurse's salary.'

'Surely your husband's insurance would have provided for the two of you?'

'I expect it would have, if he'd been insured. But young men in their twenties don't usually bother—they think they're immortal.' Her tone was wry. 'Anyway, as far as I know, most policies don't pay out for suicides.'

There was the sound of a soft oath in the quiet confines of the car, and out of the corner of her eye she saw him dart a quick glance towards her.

'I'm sorry...I didn't know...'

'Nor does anyone else at the hospital,' Hope said pointedly. 'It happened a long time ago and I've put it behind me.'

They drew into the minute car park behind the restaurant at that precise moment, and Hope was grateful for the timing. This meeting was going to be stressful enough as it was—the last thing she wanted to do was spend the evening fending off questions about Jon.

Their welcome at the Thatched Cottage was as warm as if they were personal friends of the proprietors, and in no time they were seated in comfortable armchairs with a drink in one hand and a superb menu in the other.

'So why have you never remarried?'

The question came as soon as they had made their choices, and Hope's stomach began to twist itself into a knot. If she started thinking about the emotional consequences of the end of her marriage she wouldn't be able to enjoy her meal, and she was blowed if she was going to ruin such a rare treat.

'Why have *you* never married?' she demanded, in an attempt at turning the tables on him, watching his surprised reaction with grim humour.

'*Touché*,' he acknowledged with a brief nod, but he took it in good part. 'I've never really had time to marry. Too busy working and taking care of Edward...' His voice trailed off into silence as he caught sight of the smug expression on her face and realised what he was saying. His mouth twisted in wry acknowledgement.

'Do I say snap?' Hope asked sweetly.

'It isn't easy, is it?' he admitted. 'Especially when you're single-handedly trying to take the place of two parents.'

They shared a reminiscent smile, the expression in their eyes one that spoke of old battles fought and won.

'They'll be off our hands soon, though.' There was a distinct twinkle in his eyes. 'You'll be able to start looking once you're on your own.'

'No.' Hope was definite. 'Once was enough for me. Besides, I'm too long in the tooth for anyone to want to take me on at my age...too set in my ways.'

'Rubbish! You're a very attractive woman.' His eyes travelled the length of her slender body and she reacted almost as though he had touched her, tightening her fingers around the stem of her glass to control their tremor. 'You certainly don't look old enough to be Jane's mother. You must have been the proverbial child bride.'

'I was eighteen when I married, and I was widowed and Jane was born before I was nineteen,' she detailed quietly. 'I hadn't had time to finish my nursing training so I had nothing to fall back on to support myself and my child.'

'I take it you're trying to draw parallels between your situation and your daughter's, but they're not the same—'

'They would be if anything happened to Edward before she's finished her course and found a job,' Hope broke in passionately.

'She'd have family to fall back on,' he objected. 'She wouldn't be alone in the world.'

'Neither was I, but in the long term it caused more problems than it solved. You've no idea what it can do to your mind to feel that you're dependent on charity... to be made to feel that whatever you do, whatever you achieve is always second best.'

CHAPTER THREE

HER heated reply left him silent as they were called through to the dining room to start their meal, and Hope tried hard to shut their discussion out of her head while she tasted the wine they'd chosen.

'Hope?' His deep voice broke into the silence and drew her eyes towards him; the tone suggested that it wasn't the first time he'd spoken.

The candle in the centre of the table threw wavering shadows over his face so that he seemed almost insubstantial, his eyes smoky in the intimacy of their corner, his pale hair shot with will-o'-the-wisp gleams.

'Might I suggest that in the interests of our digestive systems we leave our discussion for the end of the meal?' One eyebrow was raised, giving him an almost boyish expression, and she felt the tension between them ease.

'Well, it would be a shame to spoil a good meal.' She smiled as their first course arrived, and closed her eyes to breathe in and savour the delicious aromas. 'Mmm, it smells so good I'm almost afraid to taste it in case I'm disappointed. . .'

The meal was superb, from the delicately seasoned fish mousse to the stuffed pan-fried chicken breasts and steamed baby vegetables. The only problem was the dessert.

'I couldn't possibly eat any more,' Hope protested when confronted with an endless list of delights. 'I think I've had more this evening than I had all last week.'

'In that case perhaps you ought to be stocking up for next week,' Matthew teased. 'I promise to make you work hard enough to work it all off!'

Finally she was persuaded to try a light-as-air lemon syllabub, and ended up scraping every trace out of the bowl.

'Would you prefer to have your coffee and liqueurs in the lounge?' their host suggested when she reluctantly put her spoon down.

'That's always supposing I can get up from my chair,' Hope joked. 'That was definitely the best meal I've had in years...probably in my whole life!'

She glanced across at her companion and caught him watching her. For a second it almost seemed as if there was a softness, a warmth in his eyes, but the expression was fleeting, and when she looked again it was gone.

'If madam would like some assistance?' He came round to draw her chair back. He took her elbow in one firm hand to steady her as she regained her feet, then seemed to forget to release it as they walked through to the other room.

'Here.' He led her towards the corner of a settee, and before she realised what he was going to do he sat himself down beside her.

'Oh!' she breathed. Suddenly aware of how close he was, Hope tried to move away, to keep some distance between the two of them, but she was already sitting in the corner and his legs were so long that when he turned towards her his knees grazed her thigh...

There was an electric silence between them as their coffee was placed on the low table in front of them.

Hope racked her brains for something to talk about, but nothing came to mind. All she could concentrate on was his hard warmth brushing against her softness, while he seemed totally oblivious to their proximity.

'Cream?'

While she'd been wool-gathering he'd been filling their cups with the dark, aromatic brew.

'Oh, yes, please.' The words almost fell over each other in her haste to appear in control of herself, and she was careful to take the cup from him without allowing their fingers to touch; the state she was in she would probably spill it everywhere.

Heaven only knew why she was behaving like this. It wasn't in the least bit like her to act skittishly when a man sat beside her—she must have had too much wine...

'So.' Cup in hand, he leant back in the settee again, somehow managing to end up even closer than before, and Hope's concentration disintegrated. 'As I understand it, your main objections to Jane and Edward's marriage are that Jane hasn't finished her course and that they've got no money behind them.'

'They're also far too young,' Hope added. 'Neither of them is mature enough to take on the responsibilities of marriage.'

'They're both older than you were,' he pointed out logically.

'But age has no bearing on maturity,' she objected. 'They just seem to see a wedding as a chance for an ostentatious display. They don't seem to have grasped the vital difference between a wedding and a marriage. For heaven's sake, they've known each other for hardly a year. How can they possibly know whether they want to spend a lifetime together?'

'Well, they moved in together six months ago, so I think they've probably got a good idea...'

'What?' Hope breathed, as stunned as if she'd hit a brick wall head-first, like young Stephanie. 'What did you say?'

'That they've been living together?' He seemed puzzled. 'They told me you knew what they were doing when they asked me to help them out with half of the deposit for the flat.'

'Jane said she was going to share a flat with another girl from her college—a fellow student.' There was a strange roaring sound in her ears. 'She said she needed to borrow her half of the first month's rent but she'd let me have it back as soon as her grant came through.' She made a sound halfway between a laugh and a sob.

'Of course, she never did pay it back. Recently she seems to have developed a very convenient memory as far as money goes...' She drew in a shuddering breath and flicked the tip of her tongue over suddenly dry lips as she leant forward to deposit her cup on the table.

'Please,' she whispered, her throat tight and her eyes burning with tears she refused to shed, 'I want to go home now.' And she clasped her bag convulsively with both hands.

'Hope...are you all right? Can I get you anything?' He placed one hand over hers and the heat seemed to sear her chilled flesh.

'No.' She shook her head frantically. 'Just get me out of here...'

While he left the room to pay the bill Hope concentrated fiercely on the painting above the fireplace. The scene looked so peaceful...as though life for the people who lived in it was always smooth and predictable. Their happiness would never be destroyed by the discovery that their beautiful, honest daughter had turned into a greedy, self-centred liar...

'Hope?' Her elbow was taken in a solicitous hand and she was helped out of the settee as though she was an elderly lady. 'The car's right outside the door. You didn't bring a wrap, did you?'

She shook her head wordlessly, mortified that she needed to rely on his strength to negotiate the few steps that would take her away from the worried faces and hushed tones that surrounded her.

Outside it was blessedly dark and, knowing that no one could see her face any more, she could finally relax her shaky control.

By the time she was sitting in the deep-cushioned luxury of the car the slight quiver in her hands had become a shake—her whole body racked with it as she fought the urge to sob out her hurt. She knew he looked at her as he fastened her seat belt, but he remained silent as he set the car in motion to take her home.

'I'm sorry,' she muttered through gritted teeth when he finally drew up outside her little house. 'Thank you for . . .' She couldn't continue, reaching for the handle which would let her escape.

'Here.' He was there before her, his hand held out to help her from the car. 'Have you got your key?'

They stood together under the porch light while she scrabbled through the bottom of her bag for the elusive key and failed to find it.

'Let me,' he offered gently, holding his hand out again.

'No...I can manage,' she muttered hoarsely, just before she dropped the bag at her feet and the contents scattered into the shadows. 'Dammit,' she wailed as she ran the fingers of both hands through her hair and bent forward to search for a metallic gleam in the gloom. 'Not now!'

'I've got it.' She saw him scoop something up and straighten to his full height. 'Let's get you inside and I'll come back out to pick up the rest.'

'I can manage,' she repeated as he swung the door open. 'There's no need for you to—'

'I don't doubt that you *can* manage, but there's no reason why you should. You've had a nasty surprise and you need some time to come to terms with it.' He ushered her down the hallway. 'When I've picked them up, I'll put all your things on the hall table. You just take yourself off to bed.'

Hope wandered numbly into the bathroom, cleaning the make-up off her face and brushing her teeth by force of habit. By the time she reached her bedroom she was capable only of stripping her clothes off and leaving them in a crumpled pile on the floor before she donned the nightdress waiting under her pillow and slid into bed.

She lay there shivering, curled into a tight foetal ball and staring blankly at the light switch beside the door. She must have switched it on as she came into the room but now her strength had totally deserted her and she was wondering how she was going to manage to turn it off.

There was the unexpected sound of footsteps

approaching, and she blinked in disbelief as St Augustine's paediatric consultant walked into the room carrying a steaming mug.

'Hot milk with cinnamon and honey,' he murmured as he slid an arm under her shoulders and lifted her against the headboard. 'Can you manage, or shall I hold the mug for you?'

Wordlessly Hope held out a trembling hand, biting her lip as she had to wrap her other hand around the mug to hold it steady.

From the corner of her eye she watched him sit down on the small chair in the corner of the room, his broad shoulders and long, lean body dwarfing its dainty proportions.

She watched surreptitiously as he leant forward to place an elbow on each tautly muscled thigh, his eyes fixed on the clasped hands hanging between his widespread knees as she sipped in silence.

'Feeling better?'

Before Hope had a chance to look away he had glanced up at her, his grey-green eyes trapping hers like a rabbit mesmerised by car headlights.

'Y-yes, thank you,' she gulped, then tried to hide her reaction by burying her nose in the mug, noticing with amazement that it was all but empty.

'Do you feel up to a few minutes of conversation? Otherwise, heaven only knows when we'll get a chance to talk again.'

'I suppose so.' Hope reached out to put the empty mug on the corner of her bedside cabinet, suddenly conscious of the fact that she was entertaining a man in her bedroom wearing only a nightdress.

Stealthily she slid a little further down on her pillows,

tugging the edge of the bedclothes up until they covered all but her shoulders.

'I was a little surprised by your reaction this evening.' His deep voice sounded soothing, but his words had Hope's hackles rising. 'In the year that we've been working together you've always been eminently unflappable, no matter what chaos ensues on the ward. I've been impressed by that quality in you.'

For the first time since the fateful night they had first met Hope found herself the recipient of one of the charming smiles which he usually reserved just for his young charges.

'Thank you.' Hope was stunned by the unexpected compliment. She hadn't even realised that he'd noticed that she was on duty most of the time.

'Don't you think you might be overreacting a little over the situation with Jane and Edward?' he continued persuasively. 'Living together before marriage might not have been acceptable when we were their age, but it seems to be fairly commonplace nowadays. After all, they are legally old enough to make their own decisions.'

'I can't argue with that,' Hope agreed quietly, in spite of her growing anger. 'They are both over eighteen, and as such are legally old enough to take responsibility for their decisions. The thing I find questionable is whether either of them are in a position—either emotionally or financially—to take on that responsibility.'

'Meaning?'

'Throwing a tantrum when someone doesn't immediately agree with you is hardly a sign of emotional maturity,' Hope pointed out tightly. 'And expecting other people to foot the bill for their extravagant flights of fancy is proof that they've got ideas way beyond their own ability to pay. It's a recipe for disaster.'

'Couldn't you have brought all this up when you were discussing the wedding? Surely you could have suggested various options?'

'Hah!' Hope swallowed the bitterness with difficulty. 'Chance would have been a fine thing! The first I knew about it was a phone call out of the blue from my daughter to tell me she and Edward were getting married and to let me know the figure to fill in on the cheque for the deposit on the reception. What discussion?'

'What did you tell her?'

'What *could* I tell her? The truth, of course. That I couldn't afford it. As far as I'm concerned it is a totally ridiculous amount to spend on a wedding reception. The money would be far better spent as a deposit for a house or for starting off their married life with a nest egg for emergencies—not squandered in a couple of hours on an over-priced meal.'

There was a long silence as he digested her words, and Hope found herself fidgeting with the bedclothes, repeatedly pleating the fine cotton between her fingers while she waited for him to speak.

'What about some sort of compromise?' he suggested. 'Only we really ought to be making some arrangements fairly soon, if everything's going to be ready on time.'

'As soon as I know what shape she wants the cake I can start baking, and it will only take a weekend's work to make her dress once she's chosen the style and the fabric.'

'You're intending making them yourself?' He sounded startled. 'Have you ever done anything that ambitious before?'

'Several times.' The open scepticism in his voice stung her into speech. 'I've always made most of my own outfits and Jane's—it was the only way I could afford to keep us in new clothes.'

'Does it make much difference to the cost?' He was becoming intrigued, and his interest persuaded her to drop her guard a little.

'Depending on the fabric and style, home- made costs about a quarter of shop-bought clothes—especially for special occasions like weddings and evening dresses—and they fit!' She tried to smile, but knew that the attempt looked a little wan.

'Does Jane know that's what you're going to do? Did you get a chance to tell her?'

'She's always known,' Hope confirmed quietly. 'I told her years ago that when she eventually got married I would like to make her dress and her wedding cake—if she wanted me to. I was actually looking forward to doing all of it—including the food for the reception.'

'But you would exhaust yourself. It's a massive undertaking for the numbers the two of them are talking about.' He was aghast.

'Not if you know how to go about it. It's just a matter of organisation and. . .' She shook her head. 'There's no point in going on about it. She told me in words of one syllable that she didn't want something second best, so I'll just have to wait and see what happens next.'

The brief surge of energy which had fuelled her during their conversation drained away as she remembered the acrimonious phone call, leaving her feeling exhausted.

Her eyes closed as she leant her head back against the polished wooden headboard and her shoulders drooped.

'Will you try to get in contact with Jane?' His voice seemed to be coming from a long way away, and she barely managed to summon up the energy to shrug her shoulders and pull a tired face.

'Have you set your alarm?' There was the sound of laughter in his voice, and the warmth of it spread through Hope like an extra blanket.

'Mm-hmm.' She could feel a silly smile creeping over her face just before the welcome darkness claimed her.

'Oh, and Tommy's on his way in again,' Maggie added as she finished bringing Hope up to date on what had been happening on the ward since her last spell of duty. 'We just had a call from his GP.'

'Oh, no.' Hope could picture the six-year-old's cheeky grin clearly. He'd charmed them all on his last visit, with his cheerful irreverence. 'What's gone wrong?'

'Don't know any more than that he's had a bad week with one attack after another. Mr Benedict wants to know as soon as Tommy gets here.'

'Any bets that even a bad week won't have taken the mischief out of him?' Hope tried to cover up the jolt she'd felt when Matthew's name was mentioned by rushing into speech. She really didn't think she was ready to see him yet, not after their disastrous outing yesterday evening. It had taken her most of the day just to steel herself to come in to work this evening, in spite of her pep talks to herself.

Maggie shook her head and smiled reminiscently. 'No takers! I think that lad could power the national grid, he's got so much energy to spare!'

Hope just had time to pay a quick visit to each of her charges—filling out the information she'd read on their notes with personal observations as she chatted briefly with those well enough to talk and spoke gently to those more in need of simple encouragement.

The sound of the child-proof catches being released alerted her to the new arrival, and she made her way over to the small group entering the ward.

'Hello, Tommy.' She smiled encouragingly at the little figure in the wheelchair, half of his face obscured by the oxygen mask as he wheezed with each exhalation. 'I didn't expect to see you again.'

'We didn't expect to have to bring him here.' His father looked worn out and worried. 'He's been doing so well. . .'

'Sometimes it happens like that, Mr Lambert. A lad his age gets into everything. You can't watch him every second of the day to make sure he doesn't set an attack off.'

'You're not kidding!' his mother joked. 'If I could find the switch to turn him down to half-power. . .!'

Hope laughed sympathetically.

'If you'd like to take him over to that bed, Nurse will help you to get him settled. I'm just going to let Mr Benedict know you've arrived.'

Mentally she castigated herself for straightening her dark blue uniform and taking a swift peep in the mirror to check that her hair was tidy. She was only waiting for the arrival of the paediatric consultant to examine a patient, after all.

There was absolutely no reason why her hands should grow clammy and her pulse start to rocket at the thought that he was on his way. Just because the last time she'd seen him she'd been lying in bed in her little cramped bedroom, and he'd been sitting on the chair not three feet away...

'Sister Morgan.' His greeting was as professionally correct and impersonal as if the previous evening was a figment of her imagination, but in spite of her sinking feeling of disappointment she couldn't fault him for it. Once on the ward he was every inch the consultant, and she was the nursing sister taking care of his patients.

'Mr Benedict.' She nodded. 'Tommy's over here.' She led the way across the ward.

'Mr and Mrs Lambert.' Hope watched as his calming presence worked its usual magic. 'Any idea what this young scamp has been up to this time?'

As he questioned the troubled parents about the problems of the last week he was examining their son carefully. To ease his breathing the young lad was propped up against a pile of pillows specially sealed to minimise any allergic reaction.

Finally he straightened up.

'Your GP has given Tommy corticosteroids, but they will take a few hours to work. In the meantime, because we know from past episodes that he responds well to it, we'll give him salbutamol through a nebuliser and repeat it every two or three hours until the attack subsides.'

'How long do you think that will take?' His mother was still looking pale.

'It's difficult to say.' Matthew's forehead was pleated into worried lines. 'Especially as we don't have any idea what is triggering this latest group of attacks. He might have to stay in several days while we run some tests on him. In the meantime, if you can think of anything he's done or anywhere he's been that might have set him off. . .?'

He paused, and Hope knew that he was mentally checking every step they had already taken to make sure that nothing had been missed.

She'd been watching Tommy when it had been suggested that he might have to stay in hospital. She'd seen the expression which had crossed his face and her heart had gone out to him. With such severe reactions, he must have spent an unfair amount of his six years in hospital.

'You haven't done any decorating or changed the car?' Matthew was still trying to track down the trigger, in the hopes of eliminating it. 'If you'd been on an exotic foreign holiday he might have picked up some sort of infection or infestation that's causing it. . . What about animals? Have you or your neighbours recently acquired any pets?'

The Lamberts' negative answer faded into the background as Hope spotted Tommy's reaction. She'd almost missed it with so much of his face hidden, but when his eyes travelled stealthily around the circle of adults and shied away from meeting her eyes she was fairly sure that she knew what was going on.

'Mr Benedict,' she improvised swiftly, 'I'm sure you would be far more comfortable talking to Mr and Mrs Lambert over a cup of tea.'

Grey-green eyes met hers with the intensity of lasers

but she didn't flinch, hoping that he was intuitive enough to take the hint.

'What a very civilised idea.' His reply was charm itself as he held one hand out in invitation towards the visitors' lounge. 'Perhaps we'll think better when we're sitting down.'

Hope collared Polly as she came out of the sluice and set her to take the tray through while she returned to Tommy's bed.

'Hello, Tommy.' She sat herself down on the visitor's chair beside an unusually subdued child. 'It looks as if you're going to be spending some more time with us.'

This time she was looking for a reaction, and she saw his panic clearly.

'Don't want to stay.' His big blue eyes were so appealing that they nearly broke her heart.

'You're not frightened of staying here, are you?' She kept her voice low, so that he would realise that the conversation was just between the two of them.

'Uh-uh.' His dark tousled head demonstrated a defiant negative, then he subsided again, a single tear finding its way out from under thick, dark lashes.

'Unfortunately, if we can't find out why you're having these attacks, you might have to stay in for a long time.' She felt terrible about frightening him, and had her fingers firmly crossed out of sight while she allowed her words to sink in.

'Your mum and dad are really worried about you—especially as they don't know what's gone wrong.' She paused until he looked up at her, then fixed her eyes on his. 'Have you got any idea what's making you ill?'

She held her breath, silently praying that the good

relationship she had built up with him last time he'd been on the ward would persuade him that he could trust her.

Finally, when she had almost given up hope, there was an infinitesimal nod.

'Can you tell me?'

His big blue eyes were swimming in tears.

'It's a cat,' he wheezed, fighting for breath as his unhappiness added to the stress. 'She was going to be killed so I hid her.' He grabbed her hand. 'If I don't go home no one will feed her and she'll get ill.'

'Oh, Tommy.' She ran her free hand over his silky dark curls. 'We can't let anything bad happen to the cat, can we?'

Hope mopped up his tears matter-of-factly, knowing that even a six-year-old male would hate to be fussed. She listened while he told her the rest of the tale in fits and starts, and calmed him down by promising to take on the job of breaking the news about the hidden lodger to his parents.

When Hope pushed open the door to the small lounge Mr and Mrs Lambert were obviously just as perplexed as when they'd left the ward, the two of them still trying to suggest what might have gone wrong.

Matthew Benedict's piercing gaze sought her face as soon as she stepped into view, a silent question winging its way towards her.

'I think Sister Morgan has solved the puzzle.' He broke into the deliberations, a secretive smile lifting the corners of his mouth for a brief second before he had it under control again.

'Mr and Mrs Lambert, if you go into your garage you'll find a cardboard box in the corner beside the central heating boiler.' Her calm words riveted the young couple's attention. 'Inside you'll find a rather bedraggled cat—'

'A cat!' Mr Lambert broke in, amazed.

'As far as I can gather, she was going to be disposed of in a less than humane way. Your son rescued her and has been trying to take care of her without you knowing...'

There was silence for several seconds before Matthew's deep chuckle broke the astonished tension.

'Well, how can you be cross with a genuine hero?' he demanded. 'He saved the cat's life even at the risk of his own.'

The tense atmosphere in the room had disappeared into smiles. This, at least, was something known, something which could be dealt with.

'Well done.' His deep voice reached her as she was about to follow the Lamberts back to the ward. 'What on earth made you suspicious? His parents were adamant that Tommy wasn't in contact with any animals.'

'Intuition.' She smiled back at him over her shoulder. 'It comes with being a mother.'

'Mother?'

Hope's heart didn't know whether to take off and fly or sink without trace when she finally heard Jane's voice on the other end of the phone.

Crossing the fingers of her unoccupied hand tightly for luck, she snatched a quick breath.

'Jane! How have you been?' She swallowed to try to ease the tightness in her throat. She loved her daughter so much, and it was like having an amputation without the benefit of an anaesthetic to be at odds with her like this.

'We're OK,' she said off-handedly. 'Look, we've thought about what you said, but we've decided what sort of wedding we want and we're going to pay for it ourselves.'

There was a long silence while Hope repeated the words in her head, but she was determined that she would give her daughter no excuse to end this call in a self-righteous temper.

'If that's what you've decided, dear. It's your choice.' It was an effort to keep her voice calm and even, especially as her pulse was racing. 'Does that mean you want to organise your own dress and cake?'

'If that's what you want me to do.' The once-musical voice was hard and unforgiving.

'No, dear. It's *your* choice,' Hope insisted quietly. 'You've always known that I'm willing to make your dress and your cake if you want me to.'

'Well, in that case, yes, please.'

'Fine.' Hope managed to sound encouraging, but she didn't know how long she would be able to hide her real emotions. 'As soon as you've seen a design you like, send me a picture and a list of your measurements. I'll let you know how much fabric you'll need, so you can go and choose it, then we can arrange a weekend for you to come home while I fit it. And what about your bridesmaids?' Hope continued. 'How many will there be and what will they be wearing?'

'I'm only having Liz and Anne. You know...my friends from college. Their dresses are the same basic style as mine, but they'll be able to wear them as evening dresses afterwards. We thought burgundy-coloured shot silk would be a good idea.'

'What about the cake? If there are going to be less than fifty people, you'll only need—'

'We've decided we want three tiers of fruitcake with marzipan and fondant paste icing. The bouquets are going to be burgundy and ivory roses and freesias with trailing ivy, so you could do the decoration on the cakes to match.'

By the time her daughter rang off Hope was sitting in the corner of her settee feeling as if she'd been flattened by a steamroller.

'Compromise, the man said,' she muttered to the ceiling as she mentally totted up the cost in ingredients and time to which she'd just calmly committed herself. 'And that doesn't include making two evening dresses and a wedding dress.' She shut her eyes and groaned. 'If I get through this wedding without murdering someone, it'll be a miracle!'

CHAPTER FOUR

'WHAT on earth have you got in there? Bricks?' Doris demanded as Hope staggered out of the lift the next day, loaded down with carrier bags.

'Shopping,' she said breathlessly as she struggled to stuff the bags into her locker. 'I didn't have time to take it home before it was time to come on duty.' She pulled a couple of paper towels out of the dispenser and wet them under the cold tap before holding them over her face. 'Oh, that feels good,' she moaned.

'Would a cup of coffee help?' Doris offered.

'It could possibly be responsible for saving my life,' Hope quipped. 'Now all I need to do is work out how to cram eight hours' sleep into the next fifteen minutes and the world will be a wonderful place.'

Doris was laughing as she went to get the promised coffee, leaving Hope muttering that she wasn't joking.

It had taken several hours of concentrated mathematics to work out and total up the precise ingredients she would need to bake three fruitcakes in the appropriate graduated sizes.

A quick glance at the prices on half-empty packages already in her store cupboard had sent her on a rapid trip to the bank first thing this morning when she had realised that she had nowhere near enough cash in her purse to cover that amount.

'Now it's all down to baking the things,' she muttered as she dried her face and applied a quick layer of moisturiser to counteract the drying effect of the warmth necessary on the ward.

'Sister! Sister Morgan!'

The first voice to try to attract her attention as she entered the ward was Tommy's, his hoarse whisper and beckoning hand drawing her as irresistibly as his pleading blue eyes.

'Hello, Tommy. How are you feeling today?'

'Great! Can I ask you something?' His rapid change of subject was evidence that his health was the least of his concerns.

'What do you want to ask me?'

'Have you got a cat?' He fixed her with an intent stare which would have done an interrogator proud.

'No. Why?' Suddenly her brain caught up with her mouth. 'Oh, no, you don't, young man. I'm not getting you out of hot water by taking on that cat you rescued.'

'No. Not *that* one.' His voice was indignant. 'She's mine.'

'So why did you want to know if I've got a cat?'

'Because she had babies in the night. Five of them.' He held up one hand with the fingers spread wide. 'Mum and Dad said I can keep the mummy cat, but I've got to find good homes for her babies as soon as they're old enough to leave the mummy.'

'Are you sure your parents said you could keep the mother cat?' Hope's heart went out to him, worried that he was setting himself up for a major disappointment. 'You've been having bad attacks ever since you rescued her, and that could be dangerous.'

'Dad said I was ill because I was sitting on dusty cement beside the gas boiler, and he thinks that when Rambo's had a bath I won't have any problem.'

'Rambo?' Hope bit the side of her cheek to stop herself laughing. 'I thought Rambo was a man?'

'Yes, but my cat's going to be as strong as Rambo when I finish looking after her.'

Hope smiled her agreement and escaped while he was still thinking about his choice of name for the mother cat. With any luck he would have recovered from his asthma attack and be on his way home before he remembered that he hadn't persuaded her to take on one of the kittens.

'Ben.' Hope beckoned the charge nurse to follow her into the office. 'Do you know anything about Tommy's cat?'

'Who *doesn't* know about Tommy's cat?' Ben Overton chuckled as he propped himself against the nearest wall, his head nearly level with the top of the door. 'I think he's tried the hard sell on every single member of staff. I'm expecting him to start accosting parents and visitors any minute now!' He laughed down at Hope from his great height, the epitome of a gentle giant.

'What's the story about the mother cat? Is it true his parents have said he can keep it?'

'There's some hard bargaining going on as far as I can tell. His mother has had a word with the next-door neighbours, and apparently they've agreed to have the cat if Tommy's too sensitive to it to have it in his own home.'

'Thank God for that.' Hope sank into the chair behind her desk, nearly disappearing behind the mound of paperwork waiting for her attention. 'Poor little scrap has really set his heart on it.'

'If the patients only knew what I know about you,'

Ben said teasingly as he shouldered himself upright and turned towards the door.

'What do you mean?' Hope demanded. 'What do you know about me?'

'That you're soft as butter...a real push-over as far as your patients are concerned. If they realised it, they'd run rings around you... Oops! Sorry, sir.' As he turned to leave the room Ben narrowly avoided ploughing into Matthew Benedict.

'Good morning, Charge Nurse.' His voice was tranquillity itself. 'You surely can't be talking about our pure-steel-to-the-core Sister Morgan?'

Hope saw Ben blink at the unaccustomed banter, then he grinned. 'The very same,' Ben agreed. 'Terrifies the lot of us to keep us all in line!' He flicked Hope a cheeky salute and ducked out of sight.

A strange silence fell over the room once the two of them were left alone, each of them surreptitiously looking at the other until their eyes accidentally met.

'How are—?'

'Have you—?'

They laughed and the tension was broken.

'I was only going to ask how you were. You're looking tired.' Matthew's eyes gleamed silver under the artificial light as he examined her face.

'Thank you. That makes me feel much better.' Hope pulled a reproachful face. 'Especially as I've only just come on duty.'

'I heard from Edward last night. Apparently Jane phoned you?'

'Yes. She caught me almost as soon as I arrived home. They want me to make the cake, and Jane's going to send me a picture of the dress she wants so I can start drafting the pattern.'

'So you're happy with the way it's being organised now?'

Hope's smile died as she remembered the edgy tone of the conversation. She had an uncomfortable feeling that she had missed something important...

'It's certainly not the wedding I was expecting her to have,' she said diplomatically. 'It seems such a shame that they had to cause so much upset...so unnecessary.'

'Well, let's hope it all runs smoothly from now on.' His relief was palpable. 'They've told you they've chosen a less costly venue for the reception?'

'No. I didn't ask any more than the details about the dress and the cake. No doubt they'll let me know in due time.'

Their conversation was ended by the imperious summons of the telephone, and the calm oasis in their day disappeared with the information that a new admission was on her way up to the ward.

'Alexia Pickering has arrived at reception,' Hope said as she put the phone down. 'She's diabetic and due for surgery tomorrow.'

'Ah, yes. Severely enlarged tonsils and repeated bouts of strep infections.' He drew the details apparently effortlessly from his encyclopaedic brain.

'That's the one.' Hope shook her head in amazement. 'She's come in this morning so we can get her stabilised ready for the surgery tomorrow morning.'

'She'll have had her normal breakfast and insulin before she came in?'

'She should have. It was on the list of instructions

the parents were given, but I'll check as soon as they arrive,' she confirmed. 'Tonight she'll only get short-acting insulin before tea, and she'll go to bed with an infusion of fluids and insulin.'

'I'll give her a check as soon as she arrives, to make sure she's not harbouring any infection, then you can take blood for haemoglobin, electrolytes, urea, glucose and grouping.' He reeled off the tests he needed and Hope noted them on her check-list.

'Have you seen Tommy today?' She looked up from her notes.

'Yes.' He gave a rusty chuckle as his eyes went to the view of the ward through the observation window and the lively young boy holding an animated conversation with his bed-bound neighbour. 'I managed to escape without promising a home for one of the kittens.'

'This time,' Hope warned. 'He'll keep trying to persuade you until he's well enough to go home.'

'Thank goodness it doesn't look as if that will be so far away. He made a remarkably swift recovery once he was removed from the environment which was triggering the attack.' He shook his head. 'The resilience of children never ceases to amaze me.'

'You really enjoy your work, don't you?' Hope said softly, her words an observation rather than a question as she watched the expressions crossing his face. 'You've got a good way with the children. They instinctively know that you care.'

'Thank you.' Hope was amazed to see a hint of colour run endearingly across his cheekbones. She hadn't realised that her compliment would embarrass him, and found the idea strangely attractive.

'It's a shame you haven't had children of your own,'

she added daringly. 'You'd have made a good father.'

'To all intents and purposes I've had to be a father to Edward.' His expression was sombre. 'My brother and his wife were killed when he was ten and he's been living with me ever since.'

'It's not the same as having a real family, though,' Hope admitted sadly. 'I've had Jane to myself all her life, and I've often thought it would have been wonderful to have shared her upbringing with someone who would have loved her too.'

'She must have been very young when your husband died. Does she remember him at all?'

'He didn't know I was pregnant when he died,' Hope said, knowing that the flat inflection of her voice would discourage any further questions. She had practised saying the sentence in just that way especially so that people wouldn't ask. There were some things she still couldn't bear to talk about.

To her relief, Matthew barely had time to confirm that as far as he was concerned Alexia was fit enough for surgery the next morning when he was called away to a patient in the accident department. Hope breathed a sigh and welcomed the physiotherapist for her session with Stephanie Plews.

'I'm really pleased with her progress,' Marika Sadowska reported, her dark eyes gleaming as she helped the young girl demonstrate her new skills. 'Even yesterday Stephanie couldn't grip my hand so hard, and today she can stand up so straight that she is nearly as tall as I am!'

It wasn't just her boundless enthusiasm and encouragement for her charges which made Hope smile but the fact that at just a shade over five feet it wouldn't take much for *most* people to exceed her height.

Hope was able to give whole-hearted approval of the hard work Stephanie was putting into her own recovery and continue on her way around the ward with a smile.

'Sister, how many days did Mr Benedict say Susan Allardyce had to stay in?' Polly Turner queried when Hope reached the three-year-old's bed. 'Her mum's having a lot of trouble with late pregnancy, and she's finding it difficult to cope with the to and fro while she tries to keep this monkey nailed to the bed.'

'He said thirty-six hours,' Hope confirmed when she'd consulted his notes. 'But all her tests are back, so, as it's causing so much stress for her mum, I'll see what he says about letting her go home soon.'

'Thanks, Sister. I'll tell Mrs Allardyce—as soon as she gets back from the loo!'

'As long as you're not trying to get rid of her for the sake of a quiet life,' Hope teased.

'I wouldn't dream of such a thing.' Polly's grin was wide enough to show a pair of engaging dimples.

Hope turned to make her way to the side-ward. Cheryl had returned from Intensive Care earlier this morning, after her second trip to Theatre.

'How's she doing, Ben?' Hope murmured as she glanced at the list of observations.

'Brilliant!' He smiled down at her as he stroked the back of the solemn seven-year-old's hand reassuringly with one long finger. It was almost the only visible place he could touch that wasn't grazed or didn't have an IV line attached. 'Every time I check her she's getting stronger. At this rate she's going to be stronger than I am, and we'll have to swop places so she can look after me!'

'Good.' Hope was pleased to see that his nonsense had drawn a brief smile from their little charge. 'I don't think it will be long before we can move her out to the ward to join everyone else.'

As she watched the blue eyes sought her own with a look of entreaty.

'Please. . .' she whispered, the bruises on one side of her face making speech difficult.

'What is it, poppet?' Hope moved closer to the bed and bent down so that their faces were level. 'What do you want?'

'Maureen?' she mumbled.

'Your sister?' Hope queried, and the wan figure murmured her assent.

'Where's Maureen?' The words were hard to form. 'Is. . .is she. . .dead?' A big fat tear rolled out of the corner of her eye and trickled into her hair.

'No, Cheryl!' Hope was horrified. How could the poor child not have been told that her sister was doing well? Or perhaps she *had* been told but her drug-induced haze had prevented her from understanding. 'Maureen is out in the ward and she's getting better.' Hope put every ounce of conviction into her voice, but the youngster looked unconvinced.

'Shall I send Charge Nurse to bring her here so you can see her?' Hope offered, realising that mere words were not going to be enough.

'Please!' The expression in Cheryl's eyes drew a lump to Hope's throat.

'You. . .' Ben paused to clear the frog in his own before he continued. 'You don't mean to tell me that you want me to use my puny muscles to push your sister's bed all the way in from the ward? I'll be exhausted! I thought you were my friend...' His voice faded as he left the room.

'He's silly...' Cheryl looked brighter already as she lay with her eyes fixed expectantly on the doorway.

'But nice,' Hope added, and smiled when she heard the absent-minded 'Mm-hmm' of agreement.

'I think I can confidently predict that Cheryl's recovery rate will increase from now on,' Ben murmured as he and Hope stood to one side while the two sisters gingerly held hands and wept tears of relief.

'If only we had some way of reading their minds,' Hope sighed. 'We'd have been able to spare her hours of torment if we'd realised she believed her sister had died.'

'Every time you think you've covered everything, something like this comes along and you realise that you haven't,' Ben admitted ruefully.

Just before Hope was due to come off duty she had a phone call.

'Doris here, Hope. You're going to murder me when you see me, because I'm going to be late.'

'How late?' Hope managed the question with a pleasant tone but she'd rather have groaned.

'I'm not sure.' Her colleague's voice sounded quite unsteady the more she heard of it. 'I got in the car to come to work but when I went to reverse it out of the garage I put it into the wrong gear and I've driven it through the back wall of the garage...'

'Oh, Doris!' Hope gasped. 'Are you all right? Did you get hurt?' She felt quite guilty for her earlier impatience.

'I'm a bit shaky, but I'm waiting for a man to come to cover the hole.'

'Does that need doing straight away?' Hope had visions of waiting hours for tardy workmen.

'Unfortunately, yes. Because the back wall of the garage is part of my kitchen, and if I leave it like this it's an open invitation to burglars, if you'll excuse the pun!'

'How bad is the damage?' Hope glanced at the fob-watch pinned to the front of her uniform while she tried to calculate how many hours it was until she could reasonably expect to see her bed.

'About the size of— Hold on. He's here,' Doris interrupted herself. 'I'll be with you as soon as I can.' And the phone clattered in Hope's ear.

In the end she was three hours late arriving home with her shopping bags full of the expensive ingredients for her daughter's wedding cake.

She struggled to carry the load in from the car in one journey, and nearly fell full-length in her hallway when she didn't see the envelopes lying on the floor from a late postal delivery.

'All I need is a broken arm,' she said shakily as she stepped carefully over the slippery pile and continued into the kitchen.

By the time the kettle had boiled she had lined her purchases up beside her kitchen scales, hating the cluttered look they gave to the usually pristine room.

'I'll have to put up with it until the cakes have been made,' she muttered as she draped a clean teatowel over the packages. 'There just isn't room in my cupboards.'

She made a cup of tea to go with the quiche and fruit salad she planned to eat, and carried the laden tray towards the sitting room. A quick detour by the front door let her scoop up the offending mail, and she settled herself in her favourite seat.

'Bills and more bills.' She riffled through the pile and groaned as she saw the logos on the envelopes. 'Why do they all have to arrive in the same month?'

She was just about to put them on one side so that they didn't spoil her meal when she recognised her daughter's handwriting.

'Jane. . .' she murmured happily, and smiled in anticipation as she slit the envelope open. She didn't often have letters from her, and in view of the bad atmosphere there'd been between them recently she was delighted that she'd taken the time to write.

She picked up her cup of tea and settled back into the corner of the settee to read.

Within seconds the happy smile had become tight-lipped hurt as she scanned the curt note.

Her daughter had found a commercial pattern which closely resembled the dress she wanted. All Hope would have to do was change the clumsy sleeves and redesign the body so that it would look slimmer over the hips and wouldn't gape at the neckline.

She'd seen the fabric she was going to have—a pure silk guipure—and if Hope could let her know as quickly as possible how many yards she'd need for the bride's dress and for the two bridesmaids' she'd be able to get it straight away.

'Oh, Jane, this isn't like you,' Hope breathed as she fought back tears and the single sheet of paper fluttered out of her numb fingers and came to rest on the carpet at her feet. 'Why have you changed so much—and all for the worse. . .?'

She struggled tiredly out of the corner of the settee and carried the tray back out to the kitchen, her appetite gone.

It took all her off-duty time for the next week to work on the pattern for the dresses, with the furniture in her small sitting room pushed out of the way so that she could use the full width of the floor space.

Finally she had worked out the necessary information, and dialled Jane's number to let her know.

There was no answer, even though Hope tried at half-hour intervals right up until she got ready for bed. Even then she couldn't settle, coming back out to the sitting room to use up her nervous energy by shifting the furniture back to its rightful position.

'One last time,' she told herself as her finger hovered over the redial button, and she listened to the electronic clicks and bleeps as the system tried to connect the call.

'At last!' She congratulated herself on her persistence as she heard the ringing tone answered.

'Jane and Edward are not available at the moment...' the mechanical voice intoned into Hope's shocked ear, and she was so stunned that she nearly missed the prompt to speak.

'Hello, Jane...' God, she hated these things! She could never think quickly enough to stop her words coming out as an incomprehensible garble—and that was on a *good* day.

How she managed to relay the figures she'd jotted on her notepad without making a complete mess of them she'd never know—especially as she was still reeling from the silent rejection this message meant.

Ever since Jane had gone away to college she and

Hope had developed the system of pressing the number code on the telephone whenever they arrived home to check the identity of the last person to call while they'd been out.

Hope hadn't realised that Jane now had an answerphone because it hadn't been intercepting her calls all evening.

The fact that it had been switched on since Hope had last tried to contact her spoke volumes.

Hope switched the light off and went to bed, trying hard to be philosophical about the situation—but it was grim.

At least she could console herself with the fact that she had given her daughter the information she needed as swiftly as possible. What happened next was up to her.

'It's going to be another very long day.' Maggie Philp sighed and blew a stream of air towards the fine curls sticking limply to her forehead. 'I hate it when the weather throws one of these scorchers at us without any warning. At least it could have waited until it was my day off!'

'It makes it very hard on the patients who can't move about,' Hope agreed wanly with the bouncy staff nurse, finding it impossible to dredge up the energy to be wholehearted about anything after nearly a week of poor sleep.

'What's the matter, Hope?' There was concern in Maggie's quiet question as she followed her into the office. 'You've been looking like something the cat's dragged in for days now.'

'Thanks a lot.' Hope tried to sound insulted, but she knew that the comment was nothing less than the truth.

'Anything I can do to help?'

'Nothing.' Hope shrugged as she settled herself behind the desk for another paperwork marathon. 'Just a bit of a problem with Jane. It'll probably blow over.'

'Jane? A problem?' Maggie was genuinely dismissive. 'You don't know how lucky you are to have her. She's an absolute gem.'

She used to be, Hope silently agreed. Perhaps her brain has been taken over by aliens, and that's why she's changed so much. . .

It felt strange to see Matthew Benedict going about his normal activities on the ward—almost as if she was watching an uncannily accurate double of the man who would soon be related to her daughter. In his hospital persona he was the member of the paediatrics staff at St Augustine's that she knew least about.

When she thought about it, she was closer to almost any of the staff on the ward than she was to him—had known them longer and worked side by side with them on a daily basis—and yet the two of them had a connection which, in a matter of weeks, would make them theoretically the closest.

Much as she fought against this strange new awareness, she caught herself waiting for his familiar figure to stride into view, and, when he was on the ward, she found herself watching his every move.

There was a new fascination in seeing the way he dealt with their young charges—his normally impassive face full of expression as he sympathised, encouraged and teased by turns.

It didn't matter how frightened or surly they were when they arrived, by the time they were well enough to leave they idolised him. . .and it was the same for the staff. It seemed as if the very fact that he expected them to do their utmost for every patient was enough to have them going all-out to earn his approval.

To her chagrin, Hope realised that she was no different from the rest, and she wondered how she could have been so unobservant that she'd never realised it before.

For the last year she had worked as a key member of the team he had drawn around him and had never realised that there was an extra spring in her step when he was on the ward, an awareness that he was an important part of her existence as he came and went around the department.

'Good morning, Sister.' Hope jumped guiltily as his deep voice broke into her astounded realisations. She turned to find his familiar lean form propped on the only free corner of her desk, one foot swinging idly, and she was swept by another startling perception that nearly made her gasp aloud at its implications.

In the last year she couldn't remember a single time when Matthew Benedict had come on the ward that she hadn't been forced to acknowledge his presence in some way.

Most times this had taken the form of a direct greeting, accompanied, more often than not, by a request for 'just a quick cup of coffee'.

Even when life was more fraught there had still been a meeting of eyes, no matter how fleeting. The only thing she didn't know was whether the instigation of this awareness was due to her appreciation of him or vice versa.

'Unless you've got any disasters to report, I've just got time for a quick cup of coffee. Have you got time to join me?'

Hope stifled the grin which threatened to spread over her face as his words so nearly repeated her thoughts, then paused as she realised the one thing she had forgotten about these events: he always invited her to join him while he drank his coffee, almost as if her presence was part of the enjoyment.

'Problems?' he queried when she sat contemplating the mug clasped between both hands.

'What makes you think that?' Hope played for time, knowing that there was no way she could tell him what she'd been thinking about.

'Oh, nothing much,' he said dismissively. 'Just the fact that you're holding that mug as if you're frozen to the core when the rest of us are all but melting with the heat!'

Hope ducked her head to look at her fob-watch in the hope that he wouldn't see the heat of embarrassment crawling up her cheeks.

'Well,' she managed to croak, 'at least I'm half-day today. When I get home I'll be able to open all the windows wide to cool me down.'

'Not fair,' Matthew groaned, looking at his own watch, the stainless steel band gleaming dully against his skin as he dragged his shirt-cuff back with one finger. 'I won't get out of here until at least six. . .'

As she shut the oven door late that night Hope was still mentally replaying the relaxed give and take of that conversation.

'Since when has he been coming into the office and chatting?' she mused aloud as she finished washing up the last of the utensils and put them away.

'When he first came to St Augustine's he was the

original iceman.' She remembered the frosty glare he'd delivered with those stunning grey-green eyes. 'I wonder when he started thawing?'

She draped a clean teatowel over the cake which was destined to be the smallest of the three tiers of the wedding cake, and slid the cooling-rack to the back of the work surface to make room for the second cake, which was nearly ready to be taken out of the oven too.

'Phew!' She pulled at the neck of her clammy T-shirt and blew down the front in a vain attempt to cool herself. 'It was all right cooking in here when I could have all the doors and windows open,' she muttered to herself as she poured another tall glass of iced water. 'But once it got dark there was far too much flying nightlife coming in for my liking.' She shuddered at the memory of the kamikaze insects, and glanced up at the large face of the kitchen clock.

'Midnight!' she groaned, knowing that it would be some time yet before the largest cake was ready to come out of the oven and not daring to go to bed for fear that she wouldn't hear the alarm and it would be ruined. She couldn't afford either the time or the money to replace it, so she would just have to grit her teeth and make sure she got it right first time.

Dragging herself out of bed the next morning after only four hours of sleep wasn't easy—especially after the preceding week of poor nights.

'Well.' She lifted off the protective cloths which had covered the cakes while they were cooling and stood back to admire them before she shut them safely away into airtight tins. 'I'll just have to draw my energy from the satisfaction that the cakes are made and they're perfect.'

A quick shower and a cup of coffee helped her to focus her thoughts, and she was just about to pick up the car keys when there was a ring at the front door.

'I am so sorry to have forgotten about this,' her elderly neighbour apologised, his normally cheerful face quite doleful as he held out a parcel.

'What is it, Mr Andreas?' Hope was puzzled.

'Yesterday, the postman he asks me if I will deliver to you the parcel, but then my daughter brings her boys to visit their grandfather and—poof—it goes right out of my head. I am so sorry.'

Hope took the time to reassure him that a delay of one day was no problem before she went back inside the house to discover what the heavy package contained.

'It's from Jane,' she murmured in amazement when she recognised the handwriting. 'What on earth. . .?' She hurried through to the kitchen to use her household scissors to attack the string.

When she finally unwrapped the layers of thick paper and opened them out she was confronted by the rich jewel-tones of burgundy shot silk.

'The bridesmaids' fabric,' she whispered, and lifted the folded length of it to reveal a second cloth the colour of rich cream. A piece of paper fluttered to the floor and she pounced on it eagerly, smoothing it open to find three columns of measurements, one for each bridesmaid and one for the bride, and a date, underlined, just two weeks away—apparently the date she intended coming down to have the dress fitted.

Hope turned the paper over, but there wasn't a single word of greeting or gratitude from her daughter, and she felt her heart sink inside her like a stone.

CHAPTER FIVE

'AT LEAST I know she received my phone call,' Hope muttered sarcastically as she parked her car in a bay close to the paediatric department. For the first time since this whole nightmare began she was angry beyond tears.

'How *dare* she treat me like that?' The words emerged through clenched teeth as she walked towards the building. 'I'm her mother—the person who's spent the last nineteen years working her socks off and going without so that her precious daughter can have the best of everything...'

Hope stopped her tense monologue when she noticed two hospital groundsmen eyeing her in a very worried way, and dragged the corners of her mouth up in a grim parody of a smile. She wasn't really surprised when it wasn't returned, the two of them glancing quickly at each other and hurrying away in the opposite direction.

Suddenly the humour of the situation hit her, and Hope started to chuckle. Unfortunately this, too, earned her worried stares, this time from the other occupants of the lift, which only made her laughter harder to control.

By the time she reached her desk on the paediatric ward her stomach muscles were aching so much that she had to lean forward and wrap her arms around herself for relief.

'Hope?'

Even Matthew's unaccustomed use of her first name on the ward wasn't enough to break the over-emotional spell.

'Hope...speak to me.' His voice sounded urgent. 'Are you ill?' He grasped her shoulders to try to draw her upright, but it wasn't until he caught a glimpse of her face that he realised what was wrong with her.

'That must have been a good one. Are you going to let me in on the joke?'

Hope knew that she was edging towards hysteria, but she couldn't seem to find any way of stopping. She was just so tired, so hurt, so angry... And those people's faces had been so horrified, so funny as they'd quickly averted their eyes and hurried away...

'Sweetheart.' The deep voice was a husky murmur in her ear as she was suddenly captured in two strong arms and pulled tightly against the full length of the consultant paediatrician.

That stopped her.

'Oh!' she gulped, shocked into silence as she gazed into grey-green eyes at extremely short range and found, much to her surprise, that they weren't in the least bit cold or forbidding. In fact they were warm and compassionate and worried and...

'Good grief!' Hope suddenly realised where she was—where *they* were—and flung herself backwards out of his arms in panic, shooting a horrified glance towards the large glass window facing onto the ward.

'Did anyone see us?' she whispered, not daring to look in his direction.

'Would it matter if they had?' The calm rejoinder brought her head up in a hurry, and their eyes clashed almost audibly.

'What do you mean? Of *course* it matters. That's not the sort of behaviour expected from consultants and ward sisters.'

'Even when the consultant in question is trying to take care of the ward sister in question?'

'It isn't a joking matter.' Hope wrung her hands together in her agitation. 'St Augustine's has certain professional standards to maintain, and it can't allow the staff to—'

'Hope?' His quiet murmur stopped her speaking far faster than a shout from anyone else.

'Yes?'

'What's the matter?'

The simple question came with such a caring expression that all Hope wanted to do was walk back into his arms and feel them wrap tightly around her again while she pillowed her head on the tempting width of one broad shoulder.

'Oh, Matt.' She was dimly aware that she'd used his nick-name for the first time, but it didn't seem to matter any more. 'If you've got about a year I might have time to tell you,' she sighed.

'So, if you're feeling so low, what on earth had you laughing like that?'

'You had to be there,' she muttered, embarrassed beyond belief when she realised what an idiot she had made of herself.

'Try me?' he challenged, and sat down on the corner of her desk with his arms folded across the width of his chest as though he had all the time in the world.

'Well. . .' Hope didn't really know where to begin, but she had a horrible feeling that once she began she wouldn't be able to stop.

'I've been using my off-duty time to draft the patterns for the bride's and bridesmaids' dresses so that Jane could get her material, and then she wouldn't ring me so I had to leave a message. . .' Her throat thickened at the memory.

'And yesterday I baked the three tiers of the wedding cake, but the bottom layer is so big that I had to stay up to take it out of the oven at the right time, so I didn't get much sleep—'

'How much?' he interrupted.

'A-about four hours.' Hope blinked at the fleeting anger she saw in his eyes but she had to continue, had to get it all out.

'Then, this morning, Mr Andreas delivered the parcel, and it was such gorgeous material, but she hadn't even put a note in it. Just the lists of measurements and the date she's decided to come down for me to fit her dress.' She drew in a deep, shuddering breath, proud that she was managing to stay in control.

'That's when it hit me.' She flicked a glance up at him and her eyes were caught by the intensity of his. 'I suppose it's because I'm tired, but suddenly I was so angry that she could do such a thing and I. . .' She bit her lip and pulled a face. 'I was talking to myself as I was driving into work and I forgot to stop, and two groundsmen were looking at me, and they nearly ran away from me, as if they thought it might be con—contagious. . .'

She swallowed hard.

'You should have seen their expressions.' She covered her mouth with one hand in an attempt to control the reminiscent smile. 'And then the people in the lift who caught me laughing looked as though they thought I belonged in a strait-jacket...'

For nearly a minute there was silence in the room as he held her eyes with his—a quiet, healing silence which allowed Hope to regain control of herself.

'Thank you,' she murmured on a sigh. 'I needed to get it all off my chest. I'm just sorry that you were in the firing line.'

'Who better?' he demanded softly. 'Unless the situation has changed recently, I'm still the only one here who knows about the wedding.' He paused, his raised eyebrow making his words a question, and Hope shook her head.

'I honestly never realised just how stressful weddings could be.' He sounded amazed. 'In my innocence I thought the happy couple would name the day and choose a hotel for the reception and that would be it.' He shook his head ruefully.

'I never realised that it could bring out the worst in people,' Hope admitted. 'I didn't think for a minute that someone who is supposedly blissfully in love could be so deliberately hurtful...' She blinked hard to banish the warning sting of tears.

'You need a break.' The words were decisive. 'If you're going to cope with the rest of the run-up to this wedding you need time to recharge your batteries.'

'Chance would be a fine thing,' Hope scoffed briskly as she started getting herself organised, smoothing her hands down the dark blue skirt of her uniform and retrieving her bag from the floor to lock it in the top drawer of her desk.

'And if you had the chance?' One lean hand trapped hers on top of the pile of paperwork as she reached for the first item, and her eyes flew up to meet his.

'Pardon?' Her brain was refusing to concentrate on anything but the warmth of his fingers on hers and the soft concern in his eyes.

'If you had the chance for a complete break?' He straightened up again and she missed the warmth of the contact between their hands. 'Say, a weekend of pampering?'

'In my dreams.' She heard the wistful tone in her voice as she realised that she couldn't remember how long it was since she'd been pampered—if ever. . .

'Hope, don't take this the wrong way. . .' He hesitated for a moment, as though unsure whether to go on. 'If I could arrange it for next weekend, would you allow me to treat you?'

'Treat me?' For a second it was his profession which sprang to mind and confused her. 'Oh, no.' She suddenly understood, and shook her head fiercely. 'I don't take charity from anyone. I did it once, but never again.'

'It's *not* charity,' he insisted. 'If you crack up before the wedding you'll break your daughter's heart.'

'Only if I haven't finished the cake and the dresses,' she muttered cynically, then sighed penitently. 'I'm sorry. That was uncalled for.'

'But symptomatic of your exhaustion,' he said sternly. 'I think I'll have to get tough with you and insist that I'll ban you from the department until you've taken a break. You can't take care of other people if you aren't taking proper care of yourself.'

'All right!' Hope held up her hand in surrender. 'All right, I agree.'

'Good.' He gave a smile that made Hope's heart give a startled leap. 'Which days will you be free?'

'I've got Friday and Saturday this week, but that'll be far too soon for you to—'

'Leave it to me,' he interrupted with his usual confidence. 'I'll let you know as soon as I've made the arrangements.'

Hope watched him leave the room feeling a little as if she'd been caught up by a tornado, whirled around and then dropped back down. The room looked the same, but she was afraid that nothing else was.

Her mood of cautious optimism flowed over into the whole day, and she was uncomfortably aware that she was causing one or two raised eyebrows among her colleagues.

'Had a win on the lottery?' Maggie demanded when they were grabbing a quick cup of tea during a lull. 'You're hardly the same person today.'

'Must have found someone to put a spring in her step,' Ben hinted heavily, and Hope's cheeks grew warm as she wondered if her momentary lapse when she'd come on duty *had* been witnessed after all. Had someone seen Matthew's arms around her while he calmed her down and jumped to the wrong conclusions?

'In all the time you've worked with her, have you known Hope to waste her time on men?' Maggie demanded, her mocking challenge to Ben's suggestion breaking into Hope's worried thoughts. 'She's either far too sensible to bother with any of you, or far too discriminating to bother going out with anyone on the staff here.'

If only you knew, Hope thought as a treacherous bubble of excitement lifted her spirits for the first time in days, and she hid her smile behind her cup before sending them back to work.

The task of going around the ward with the paediatric consultant she kept for herself, relishing the time spent in his company in spite of the fact that when he returned to the ward he was once again properly professionally distant.

'The ward's a quieter place since Tommy Lambert's gone home,' he commented.

'Yes,' Hope agreed with a reminiscent smile. 'But the staff are still comparing notes on the various methods he used to try to persuade them to take on one of his kittens.'

'Did anyone succumb?' His grey-green eyes were smiling into hers, and she had to force herself to break the connection before she melted into a puddle at his feet. What on earth was wrong with her today?

'Not so far as I know...at least, no one's admitting it if they did!' She silently cursed the breathless tone to her voice.

'How is Alexia Pickering doing?' He moved on to the next file. 'She was nicely stabilised by the time she came down to Theatre, and her tonsillectomy went perfectly straightforwardly.'

'Doing well,' Hope confirmed. 'She's due to come off the insulin drip today. We've been checking her blood-glucose level three-hourly.'

'Has she been complaining much about pain?'

'Just the usual moan about a sore throat, but the promise of a bowl of ice-cream soon sorted that out!'

'Bribery and corruption,' he accused with a smile.

'Works every time,' Hope agreed lightly.

'Does it?' he murmured in a husky aside. 'Perhaps it's worth trying. . .'

Hope was so shocked at the unexpectedness of the insinuation that she could hardly believe what she'd heard, and didn't dare ask him to repeat it in case she'd been right.

Her pulse still hadn't quite calmed down when he paused on his way out of the ward.

'By the way,' he said softly, 'everything's arranged for Thursday.'

'Thursday?' Hope squeaked. 'But my days are Friday and Saturday. I can't just—'

'Calm down.' He ushered her swiftly back into her office, where she swung round to face him like an animal at bay. 'You'll be leaving after work on Thursday to make the most of the two days. Can you be ready to leave straight from the hospital, or will you need to go back home first?'

'That rather depends on where I'm going,' she temporised. 'What will I need to take with me?'

'I would suggest mostly casual clothes suitable for the countryside. Perhaps something smart for the evening?' His tone was hesitant. 'I'm a bachelor. What do I know?' He shrugged exaggeratedly, making Hope laugh.

'I'll need directions,' she reminded him.

'What for? I'll be driving you down myself.'

'That isn't necessary,' Hope objected, in spite of the warm glow of pleasure the idea afforded her. 'You're treating me to this break so you shouldn't have to—'

'Exactly,' he interrupted smugly. 'It's my treat, and it starts with a chauffeur to drive you there.'

In the end she gave up arguing with him and accepted

the offer gratefully, knowing that the last thing she would feel like doing at the end of a busy shift would be navigating her way to parts unknown.

Thursday morning seemed to drag by until Hope almost felt as if she could scream with impatience, but the afternoon flew by far too fast as butterflies multiplied in her stomach.

By the time she finished handing over to Doris her hands were shaking and she felt quite sick, her face so pale when she caught sight of it in the mirror that she hurriedly attempted to apply a little colour before she went down to the car park to meet him.

'Ready?' He straightened up from his relaxed position leaning against the side of the dark green car and held out his hand for her small bag. 'Is this everything?'

'I'm only going to be away for a couple of days,' she reminded him, breathing a sigh of relief that he hadn't noticed how tense she was. 'This should be plenty.'

'Are you sure?' A frown drew his brows together. 'Most women seem to take enough for a month.'

Hope was stung by the comparison.

'You mean, most of the women *you* know,' she corrected as disappointment flooded her.

There was a taut silence while he deposited her bag on the back seat and ushered her into the front, striding swiftly round the car to let himself in behind the wheel.

He put the key in the ignition to start the engine, then paused, leaning back in his seat and tilting his head against the rest to gaze blindly into the distance.

'There haven't been that many,' he said, in a voice so low that she wouldn't have heard it if they hadn't been cocooned so closely together in his luxurious car.

'Many what?' Hope turned to look at him, slow to follow his train of thought.

'Many women,' he clarified as she watched a slow tide of colour engulf the lean planes of his cheeks. 'Not since I took Edward on. It didn't seem right somehow...'

'But—' Hope was shaken by the direction the conversation had taken '—he's twenty-one now. He must have left home several years ago, to all intents and purposes.'

'I found it...difficult to get back into the swim of things.' His smile was wry. 'I think maybe I'd been tethered on dry land too long.'

'While I never learned to swim at all.' Hope took pity on his apparent self-consciousness while revelling in the thought that he had wanted her to know that he'd been far from promiscuous in the last ten years.

They'd been travelling for several minutes before she thought to wonder why he had told her at all...

'Oh, Matthew, it's lovely!' she exclaimed when they drove round the last bend of a winding driveway and their destination was revealed.

'Apparently it was once a small manor-house,' he offered as he drew up outside the front door.

'It's perfect! Like a picture in a book.' She released the catch of her door and drew in a deep breath. 'I can smell roses.'

'There are about two acres of gardens to walk in.' His voice was muffled as he reached inside the back of the car, then straightened up to flick the door closed with his elbow. 'Ready to register? Exploring can come later.'

Hope turned from her rapt contemplation of the colourful display of flowers and went to follow him towards the entrance, only to come to a sudden halt.

'Matt? What's going on?' she demanded quietly, conscious that they might be overheard. 'Why are you carrying two bags?'

He continued walking, his voice drifting back over his shoulder.

'Why not? Don't you think I'll need a change of clothes too?'

'That's not what I meant and you know it,' she hissed as she scurried to catch up with him before he reached the door. 'You never said anything about this becoming a twosome.'

'Didn't I? I do apologise,' he said glibly, but his pace didn't waver, and Hope was forced to follow him through into the reception area.

'If you think,' Hope began militantly as disappointment squeezed her heart, 'that I agreed to this break so that you could arrange for the two of us to—'

'Good evening.' To her fury he totally ignored her to greet the young woman behind the reception desk. 'You have a reservation in the name of Benedict?'

'Yes, sir,' she confirmed as she looked up from the book with a smile. 'Two rooms. If you'd like to sign the register I'll just arrange for someone to take you up.'

Hope was silent as they travelled up in a lift cleverly concealed behind wooden panelling to disguise its modern presence. A quick glance at Matthew revealed a face every bit as stony as she had expected, and she dreaded finding out what he was thinking.

What on earth had made her assume that he had arranged some sort of illicit tryst? Why hadn't she waited until she'd found out what was really going on before she'd made such an unnecessary fuss?

Her room was beautiful, but she was hardly in the right frame of mind to appreciate it or the stunning view out across the gardens while Matthew was looking so grim.

She knew that he was standing in the corridor outside her door waiting to be taken to his own room, but there was no way that she could apologise for her mistake with the hotel employee listening to her.

Hope stood still once her door closed, trying to hear which direction they were taking on their way to Matthew's room, but the carpet in the hallway was far too thick and luxurious to allow any tell-tale sounds.

She sighed, realising sadly that she had spoilt the easy atmosphere which had been growing between them with one thoughtless assumption—as if a handsome, successful professional such as Matthew Benedict would have to resort to cheap subterfuge to spend time with a woman.

As she unzipped her bag and prepared to take out the few items she'd packed there was the sound of a key turning in the door behind her. She whirled towards the source of the noise just as it was followed by a crisp knock.

'Come in,' she called, confused by the strange sequence of events until the connecting door with the adjacent room opened to reveal Matthew's stony countenance.

'This is for you,' he said bleakly as he held out a key. 'I wouldn't want you to think that I might be tempted to force myself on you.'

'I don't... You wouldn't... Oh, Matthew, I'm sorry.' Hope pressed her lips tightly together while she tried to organise her tangled thoughts. 'I *am* sorry for what I implied. It was most unfair of me to even suggest such a thing, when you've done everything to make sure I have a relaxing break.'

She held her breath, her fingers knotting together until her knuckles went white while she waited for his reaction, her eyes focused on the harsh line of his jaw where a muscle pulsed rhythmically in time to the clenching of his teeth.

It seemed an age before she saw him release the breath he, too, must have been holding.

'Here, I still think you'd better take charge of this.' He offered her the key again, but this time there was a gleam of humour in his eyes. 'Isn't it supposed to be the woman's prerogative or something?'

'I wouldn't know,' Hope admitted, in a voice made husky by relief. 'I've never had a connecting room before. Actually, I haven't been in a hotel for...for twenty years.' She took the few steps necessary to hold her hand out for him to give her the key.

'Twenty years?' He was clearly amazed. 'Where do you usually go for holidays?'

'That was the last time I went.' She lowered her eyes at the memory of the disaster *that* had turned out to be, then banished it from her mind. 'I've managed to send Jane on some of the trips organised by the school, but with a mortgage to pay and only one wage coming in...' She shrugged.

'In which case, this break is long overdue.' His voice became brisk as he glanced at his watch. 'You've got half an hour to unpack and freshen up before they start serving dinner.'

'Yes, sir. Certainly, sir,' she mocked, her heart lighter than air.

'That's what I like to hear—instant obedience. I'll knock on your door when I'm ready to go down.' And he disappeared back into his own room, pulling the connecting door firmly closed behind him.

Hope drew in a deep sigh of relief before she turned back to her bag, pulling a face when she saw the small pile of garments she had brought with her to choose from.

'Well, I didn't know *he* would be coming with me,' she muttered, thinking of several more flattering outfits she could have brought if she'd known.

As it was, she would be going down to dinner with him wearing the same blue-grey dress he'd seen before—the one which she'd been wearing when her shock at his revelations about Jane and Edward's clandestine living arrangements had spoilt their meal at the Thatched Cottage...

Determination had her squaring her shoulders as she grabbed her wash-bag and made for the *en suite* bathroom. Tonight would be different. Tonight she would be serenity personified; nothing would be allowed to spoil their evening this time.

Matthew's knock came just as she nervously checked her lipstick for the third time, and she drew in a sharp breath, her hand flying up to cover the fluttering in her stomach.

'Idiot,' she muttered. 'There's nothing to be nervous about. You've seen him nearly every day for the last year.' And she went across to open the door.

'Matt...' Her calm greeting flew out of her head when she saw him standing there. In all the last year she had never seen him looking like this. Oh, he was always smartly dressed, but this... Her eyes strayed from the silvery gleam of smoothly brushed hair down to flawlessly polished shoes and back up again, missing none of the length, strength and power enclosed in smooth dark suiting and pristine white shirt.

'That colour brings out the blue in your eyes.' His low murmur made her realise that he, too, had been conducting an intimate survey, and she cursed the pale skin which must now be showing the result of her embarrassment.

'Thank you,' she whispered, silently berating her lack of sophistication.

'Shall we go?' His voice sounded slightly husky as he stepped back and she followed him into the corridor.

Over their aperitif they exchanged stories about their training, and by the main course they were deep into a discussion about the changing role of nursing in the hospital situation.

By the time they reached medical politics and ethics it was as if they'd been holding conversations like this for years, each testing the limits of the other's convictions at every turn.

They were so wrapped in each other's company that each course was cleared and replaced with hardly an acknowledgement, and it took a hysterical shriek from a woman at the other side of the room to alert them to the commotion going on outside their charmed circle.

'Help him!' They saw the woman leap to her feet, her chair toppling in silent slow motion onto the thick carpet. 'My husband's choking...!'

Almost before Hope realised he was moving Matthew had reached the other table, and she hurried to join him.

The distressed man was clutching his throat in the universal signal for choking, the lack of breathing sounds making it obvious that his airway was completely blocked by an obstruction.

'Stand up,' Matthew ordered briskly, his commanding voice cutting effortlessly through the wailing sounds made by his middle-aged companion as he wrapped an arm around the portly body to assist him.

'Lean forward,' he continued, and when the terrified purple-faced man complied he delivered four sharp blows with the heel of his hand between the victim's shoulderblades.

'No good,' Hope heard him mutter when the poor man still struggled for breath, and she watched as he stepped behind him and wrapped both arms around his chest just underneath his armpits, his greater height enabling him to position himself perfectly for maximum effect.

'Oh, George...' The terrified woman looked as though she might collapse too, so Hope silently placed a supporting arm around her thin shoulders.

Although she wasn't able to see it, Hope knew that the thumb side of Matthew's clenched fist was being placed over the middle of the man's sternum then grasped in his other hand before he pulled sharply, directly back towards himself.

Hope found herself silently counting the thrusts, and had reached six before there was a sudden explosion of sound and the man started coughing, a large piece of meat flying out to land by his feet.

'Oh, thank God,' the woman moaned, and sagged against Hope. 'Oh, George, are you all right?'

Matthew was lowering him back into his seat, and Hope saw him monitoring the man's breathing for a moment before he stepped back.

'He should be fine now,' he said reassuringly, smiling up towards Hope, and she felt the woman beside her straighten up and step away.

'How can we ever thank you?' She reached out to grasp Matthew's arm. 'If it hadn't been for you...' She shook her greying head.

'If you want to do something to thank me—' Matthew's smile was at its most charming '—sign both of yourselves up to do a first aid course, so that if you're ever in this situation again with someone else you'll be in a position to return the favour.'

Hope saw the woman blink, as though his words were the last thing she had expected to hear.

'Damn good idea.' A gruff voice broke into the silence as the recovering victim found his voice. 'It's the least we can do.' He held his shaking hand out towards Matthew. 'Thank you for your quick thinking.'

They extricated themselves from the dining room as soon as possible, neither of them wanting to return to their table for coffee after all the excitement.

They made their way back up towards their rooms and Hope was just regretting the sudden end to their relaxing evening when he spoke.

'I'm sorry about that.' He gestured back towards the dining room. 'I promised a relaxing weekend, and we haven't been here more than a couple of hours before we're in the thick of a medical emergency.'

'It was hardly your fault, so this time I'll have to excuse you.' She smiled her absolution.

'Have you brought a wrap or a jacket?' Matthew paused in the softly lit corridor. 'We could go for a walk in the garden while we wait for our meals to go down.'

'Yes.' She hoped that her voice didn't sound too eager. 'It's a hand-knitted Aran.'

'Well, you go in and grab it while I wait out here.' He leant back against the wall opposite her door, the light-sconce gilding his hair and highlighting the elegant bone structure of his face. 'Go on. Scoot!' he urged as he folded his arms. 'I won't wait forever!'

CHAPTER SIX

THE roses weren't the only flowers Hope could smell as she sauntered through the shadowy garden at Matthew's side.

'That smells like sage,' she commented as they passed one bed, her voice lowered almost as if she was in a church.

Matthew leant forward to sniff at it. 'I think you could be right.' He pinched off a single leaf and handed it to her. 'It looks as if a whole bed of herbs has been planted out for decoration.'

'I'd love to be able to do that,' Hope sighed. 'I have to make do with a couple of pots on the kitchen windowsill or buying them dried.'

'Until fairly recently I'd never even tried using them in my cooking—when Edward was with me all he was interested in was quantity!'

'You do your own cooking?' Hope couldn't help the surprise in her tone.

'As I like eating, it's a case of having to!' he teased. 'I found I didn't enjoy going out every evening, and instant meals get very boring very quickly.'

'There's always the hospital canteen,' Hope suggested slyly.

'Not if you value your health,' he laughed. 'It's OK just to keep the engine going until you get home, but it's not the same as a home-cooked meal.'

'Did you never think of marrying?'

'Not just to get someone to cook,' he retorted.

'I didn't mean—'

'I know.' He captured her hand and gave it a squeeze to show that he'd been joking.

Hope grew silent, relishing the warmth of his palm against hers, his fingers threaded securely between hers as if he had no intention of releasing them in a hurry.

'I was engaged when Edward came to live with me.' The words drifted on the cooling breeze, and Hope felt a shiver snake its way up her spine in spite of the fact that she was perfectly warm enough.

'Why didn't you marry her...or did you?' She suddenly realised how impertinent her assumption sounded.

'I found out the hard way that she didn't even want children of her own, let alone the task of caring for another man's child.' His words lowered the temperature of the air around them and Hope knew, even though it was now too dark to see his face clearly, that his expression was pure iceman.

'She thought she could persuade me to send him away to boarding-school on a full-time basis so he wouldn't interfere in "our" lives, but when I told her his presence in my home was non-negotiable she went onto pastures new.'

'You wanted children?' she enquired, hoping to steer him onto more cheerful topics.

'A houseful would have been nice,' he said almost wistfully. 'It's always struck me as a shame that I had an income big enough to support them and a house large enough to contain them, but I never found the woman to share them with...'

He allowed his words to die away on the breeze, and

Hope felt her throat close up at the thought of Matthew as a loving father.

Before she had a chance to get her emotions under control he turned the tables on her.

'What about you? If your husband hadn't died would the two of you have had more children?'

'No!' Her reply was instantaneous, and she couldn't help the deep revulsion in her voice as she remembered Jon.

'That doesn't sound like the Hope I know,' he teased gently. 'I know how much you love your daughter; wouldn't you have wanted other children?'

'If he'd come near me again I'd have killed him,' she vowed as the hatred she'd quelled for years erupted inside her. She snatched her hand away from his and whirled to escape, horrified by what she had revealed.

'Hope?' From the corner of her eye she saw him reach for her and she ran, her feet finding their own way along dimly perceived paths until she reached the hotel.

Slowing her pace so that she didn't excite any attention, she made her way up the main staircase, using the effort of climbing all the stairs to get herself under control.

Gratefully she unlocked her door and let herself into the sanctuary of her room, leaving the lights off while she stood shaking in the darkness.

'Hope?' The unexpected sound of the deep, familiar voice made her shriek.

'How...how did you get in here?' She fumbled for the light switch just inside the door, but before she could find it there was a click and one of the small occasional lamps came on to highlight his lean form as he stood near the open connecting door.

'I followed you into the hotel and came straight up in the lift. When I got to your door there was no answer from your room, so I came through my room to try this door on the off chance that it wasn't locked.'

'Why?' Hope flung the word at him like a weapon.

'Because I was worried about you,' he said simply, his silvery gaze full of concern. 'And I wanted to apologise for whatever I said that made you run off like that.'

'It wasn't you.' Her throat felt tight as she forced the words past the lump growing there. 'It was who. . . what you reminded me of. . .'

'Would it help if you told me?' he offered, his voice so calm and unthreatening that for the first time Hope was tempted to share the burden.

'I don't know if I can.' Her voice was husky and she couldn't stop twisting her fingers together in torment, her breathing rough and erratic as she tried to control her trembling.

'Would you rather I left you alone?' The caring words shouldn't have cut like a knife but they did.

'No!' The panic hit her. 'Please, don't go.' She held out one hand in entreaty. 'I need—' She had nearly said, I need you, but managed to stop herself in time, substituting the less revealing, 'I need. . .to tell someone. . .'

She sank onto the corner of the bed, her hands clutching at the carved wooden decoration on the corner of the old-fashioned footboard.

'What happened?' Matthew prompted gently. 'What did your husband do to you?'

Hope's breath caught in her throat and emerged as a sob, so that she could only shake her head helplessly.

'Oh, sweetheart.' It was the second time he'd called

her that, and for the second time she found herself enfolded in the blissful security of his strong arms. 'Take your time. You don't have to tell me anything you don't want to.'

Hope clenched her teeth and released her breath in a deep sigh.

'I don't want to...but I *need* to. It's almost as if it has to be exorcised...' She glanced up at him, needing to look at him but afraid that all her self-doubts must be displayed on her face for him to see. 'Does that sound stupid?'

'Not at all.' He tightened his arms around her reassuringly and settled her against his side. 'Why don't you start at the beginning? How did you meet him?'

'He was the boy next door.' She gave a brief, self-deprecating chuckle. 'Sounds corny, doesn't it? But from the day my parents moved into the house next door it was as if I had gained a big brother as well as an extra mother.'

She relaxed a little as she remembered the good days so long ago. 'I called his mother Mum almost from that first day, it just felt so right. That's why, when my parents were killed by a drunken driver coming back from the firm's Christmas dinner, I just moved in with them permanently.'

'Were you happy?' he prompted.

'Yes. His mother treated me as if I was her own daughter and Jon's little sister.'

'When did you realise you were falling in love with him?'

'I didn't,' she denied. 'Oh, I loved him because he was my family, and he'd always been there for me, but I was halfway through my nursing training with no intention of getting married for years when his mother began pushing me to marry Jon.'

'Why did she do that? Didn't she want you to choose anyone outside the family?'

'I didn't know why, just that it had become an obsession with her.' She shook her head. 'In the end she resorted to throwing their generosity towards me in my face, reminding me of how she'd taken me in when my parents died, so that I felt. . .blackmailed into it.'

'That's ludicrous.' Matthew's deep voice reverberated through his chest under her ear. 'What was the point?'

'I had no idea until after the w-wedding.' As Hope drew closer to the crux of the tale her voice began to shake. To her immense relief Matthew began to stroke her, the soothing caress running up and down her back as though she were a frightened animal.

'What sort of wedding was it? Did she rush the whole thing through in a register office to make sure you couldn't change your mind?'

'No such luck. She insisted that I had to have the white dress and the big reception. . . I can remember thinking at the time that it was almost as though she was making sure the whole neighbourhood knew we were married, as though putting on a show would make up for the fact that she'd pushed me into it.'

'What about her son? Was he going through with it because he'd fallen in love with you?'

'That's what she told me, and I was flattered and began to get excited about. . .well, about the intimate side of marriage. But when we went away after the ceremony it was as if he could hardly bear to be in the same room as me.'

'Good God! Did you ask him why?'

'He told me to ask his mother!'

'What?' Matthew leant back so that he could catch a glimpse of her face. 'What did you do?'

'I *asked* his mother,' she said simply. 'I told her that. . .that nothing had happened on our honeymoon, and she said she'd have a word with him about it.'

'And that's all she said? No explanation?'

'No. She just said everything would be all right.'

'And?'

'She went away for the weekend so that Jon and I would have the house to ourselves. . .' Hope drew in a shuddering breath as she relived that far-away day. 'I cooked him a special meal and wore the nightie the nurses at the hospital had given me as a honeymoon present.'

'What did he say?' His voice was still as calm as ever, and in spite of the tension she could feel in him his hand continued its calming caress.

'Nothing. He never said a word all the time he was beating me and then he. . .he raped me.'

'Dear God,' he breathed, his hand still at last as he cradled her head against his shoulder. 'Why?'

'Because he was a homosexual, and it was the only way he could. . .perform with a woman.'

'Didn't his mother know what he was?'

'Of course she did,' Hope said bitterly. 'It was because he'd finally told her why he'd never brought any prospective brides home that she forced me to marry him, so none of the neighbours would know. Unfortunately, *I* didn't find that out until much later.'

Somehow, as she'd been reliving that awful night, he'd slid her legs across his lap, so that now he was rocking her in his arms like a precious child.

'Oh, Hope, I'm so sorry,' he murmured, his breath stirring tendrils of hair at her temples. 'Sorry that the people who should have protected you broke your trust; sorry that they spoiled what should have been the happiest time in your life, but most of all sorry that they knowingly put you through a trauma like that. An introduction like that could have put an innocent girl off sex for life.'

Hope stiffened, and the silence that fell then was like a suffocating blanket. She tried desperately to think of something to say. Something light, something dismissive... But it was no good. He was far too astute not to have realised...

'It did, didn't it?' he demanded hoarsely, holding her away from him by her shoulders so that he could see her face. 'Those bloody people...' He shook his head, totally lost for words, but his expression was enough.

Hope had been so afraid for so long—afraid to remember the horror of that night and the week she'd spent in hospital as she'd recovered from her injuries; afraid that people would find out what had happened and blame her. Just the way Jon's mother had said they would.

Most of all she had been afraid that if she ever met a man that she could love he would turn from her in disgust if she ever told him about her past.

Then Matthew had come into her life in such a roundabout way, and for the first time she had met the one person who had given her the courage to release all the bitterness she'd kept bottled up inside—the courage to take a chance that he would understand what she had gone through.

Suddenly the relief was too much to bear, and she buried her head on his shoulder and wept.

'Shh, sweetheart,' he murmured while he rocked her tirelessly, and just hearing that precious word again made her cry all the harder—cry until she was totally exhausted and fell asleep in his arms.

It was still dark when she woke up, and she was completely disorientated in spite of the light still burning on the other side of the room.

Why had her bedroom changed shape? What had happened to her chintz curtains? And what was the heavy weight across her waist, pinning her to the bed?

The last question was the first one to be answered.

'How are you feeling?' a deep familiar voice murmured in her ear, and her head spun to face him.

'What are you doing here?' She couldn't help the outraged tone. 'Why are you in my bed?'

His chuckle made all the hairs on the back of her neck stand up as if they'd been stroked with velvet.

'I think, if you check, you'll find that we're *on* the bed rather than *in* it, and the reason I'm here is because you wouldn't let go of me.'

Hope suddenly realised that not only was his arm resting across her waist but her hand was clutching his sleeve, and she drew it away as sharply as if the contact had burnt her, her cheeks flaming with embarrassment.

'I'm sorry,' she croaked, and tried to roll away from him to the other side of the bed, only to feel his arm tighten enough to prevent her moving.

'I'm not,' he murmured as lazily as a sleepy cat. 'It's

been no hardship at all to curl up on a comfortable bed with a beautiful woman in my arms. The only fly in the ointment was the fact that she was snoring.'

'I do not snore!' Hope squawked as indignation banished self-consciousness.

'How do you know?' he challenged.

'Because. . .because I don't.' She tried to pull away again, with the same lack of success. 'Matthew, I can't get up.'

'I know.' He sounded positively smug.

'Are you going to let me get up?' She made her voice as tolerant as if he was a particularly stubborn patient.

'No.' Even his smile taunted her.

'Why not?'

'Because. . .because I don't want to,' he mimicked her earlier words. 'I'm perfectly happy just as I am.' As he spoke he rolled towards her, wrapping both arms around her until they were in contact from their toes to their shoulders. 'On the other hand—' his voice seemed to have grown deeper '—perhaps perfectly happy was overstating the situation.'

Hope looked up at him, ready to question him further, but the expression in his eyes drove the words out of her head.

'Hope?' There was gravel in his voice.

'What?' she breathed weakly, mesmerised by the dark gleam of his eyes.

'Would you mind if I kissed you?' His chest expanded sharply as she ran the tip of her tongue nervously across her lower lip.

'Why?' The pulse at the base of her throat was beating so hard that she couldn't hear herself think.

'Because I need to taste you,' he breathed as he lowered his lips to hers.

Her brain was functioning just well enough to realise that he was giving her enough time to object, and then it ceased to reason at all, every circuit concentrating on the exquisite pleasure of Matthew's fingers spearing through her hair to tilt her face just so; Matthew's lips touching hers so gently, so warmly; the tip of Matthew's tongue stroking the same path across her lips as her own had done.

'Sweetheart?' he whispered without breaking the contact between them.

'Yes?'

'Open your mouth for me...'

'Open...?' As she spoke his tongue took advantage of the fact and delved inside to find her own.

'Matthew?' Hope moaned and he paused.

'Do you want me to stop?' he demanded huskily, and she felt his body grow rigid against hers as he fought for control.

'Can...can I ask you a question?' Shyness made her words hesitant, but suddenly she knew that this was what she wanted, this was where she belonged.

'Anything,' he offered. 'You can ask me anything.' There was absolute honesty in his darkly smoky eyes as she nerved herself to speak, and he stroked his fingers gently through the thickness of her silky hair, as though to calm her for the effort.

'Would you...will you make love with me?' The words tumbled out in a rush, and she felt the shock of them hit him.

When he began to lift his body away from hers she

nearly cried aloud with the pain of his rejection and turned her head away.

'I'm sorry,' she mumbled, wishing she could just disappear. 'I shouldn't have asked such a—'

'Shh, sweetheart.' He cupped her cheek with one hand and turned her back to face him. 'Please don't tell me you've changed your mind.'

'Changed. . .?' Hope frowned her puzzlement. 'But you were turning away from me.'

'Only so that I could start getting rid of our clothes,' he whispered as he slid one hand under the opened edge of her Aran jacket. 'I want to see you. I want to touch you.'

'Oh, Matthew.' The heat rose in her cheeks and she looked away from him again.

'What's the matter?'

'I don't know what to do,' she wailed softly. 'I've got a daughter old enough to be getting married and I don't know how to make love.'

'Ah, Hope.' He pressed a gentle kiss to her forehead. 'It will be my pleasure to teach you everything you want to know.'

When Hope woke up again it was daylight, and she knew exactly where she was and exactly whose arm was holding her possessively close to his side.

Matthew, she breathed silently as she watched him sleep, his silky blond hair rumpled, his eyelashes darker blond crescents forming fan-like shadows on his cheekbones.

The muted sunlight coming through the sheer net curtains struck golden gleams from the stubble darkening his chin, and her fingers itched to feel the sexy rasp of it. Only the fact that he was exhausted and needed his sleep prevented her from exploring.

She should have been just as exhausted, but somehow the loss of the millstone she'd been carrying around her neck for nearly twenty years had put new life in her. Either that or it was the exhilaration of finally learning about the other half of herself—the feminine, wanton side she hadn't even known existed until Matthew had shown her.

'Brazen hussy.' His voice rasped in her ear as one hand came up to cup her naked breast and tease her already erect nipple. 'What were you thinking about that's getting you all aroused? I think that shows a distinct lack of gratitude. I exhaust myself all night giving her a guided tour of her own sexuality and she repays me by waking up early and starting without me...'

He ducked his head to take her nipple into his mouth and torment it in just the way that she now found irresistible.

Hope moaned and clasped his head against her, arching her back to offer the other breast for the same attention.

Already her legs were moving restlessly under the bedclothes, the sweet ache growing in anticipation as she parted them for his exploration.

'Ah, sweetheart.' He lifted his head from her breasts just long enough to take her mouth in a parody of the possession she was longing for, and she slid her hands down his sides to grasp his hips in a blatant demand.

'Please, Matthew. Now...!' And she wrapped her

legs around him and taunted him with her body until he was powerless to resist.

'Woman, you're going to kill me.' His voice was muffled by the pillow beside her head. He tried to roll away from her, warning her that he was too heavy for her, but she couldn't bear to let him go just yet and wrapped her arms and legs firmly around him.

'Ah, but what a way to go,' she murmured wickedly, with a saucy tilt of her hips to remind him that they were still intimately joined.

'Ah, but what about moderation in all things?'

'Rhubarb to moderation! You don't make me feel moderate!' She felt him chuckling. 'What?' she demanded, and prodded his ribs until he lifted his head.

'To be perfectly honest—' his eyes were full of that wicked gleam again '—I have never felt less like being moderate in my life.' He framed her face between his hands and gazed down at her. 'Hope Morgan, you are a beautiful woman—inside and out,' he declared, and kissed her so sweetly and gently that she nearly cried.

The rest of their time at the Manor passed in a haze of gentle walks in the beautiful gardens and perfect meals perfectly presented, but all it took was a meeting of grey-green eyes with blue-grey, and a certain expression in both, and the two of them were powerless to resist the lure of the lift to take them upstairs as fast as possible.

It was like magic—a time out of mind that excluded the rest of the world and all its problems.

It wasn't until she came to pack her bag at the end of their stay that Hope's feet began to come back to earth.

In the morning the two of them were due back on duty in the paediatric ward at St Augustine's Hospital, where there would be no chance of holding hands or gazing into each other's eyes.

Once they left the Manor would the magic spell be broken? Had it all been a fluke, brought about by the release of stress and tension?

She wished that she had enough experience to know, but it wasn't the sort of thing she could ask—not even Matthew.

The journey home was even quieter than the outward one, the car's expensive sound system surrounding them with soothing classical music.

As she sat quietly beside him Hope was very much afraid that Matthew was using the time to try and find a way to let her down gently.

Her heart was already aching with the loss of the closeness they'd found at the Manor, but long years of self-reliance had her squaring her shoulders for yet another challenge.

'Thank you so much, Matthew,' she murmured as he pulled up outside her little house and she reached out to open the car door. 'You'll never know how much these last two days have meant to me. I'll never forget them.' She knew the words bore the stamp of utter sincerity because she meant them with all her heart.

'It's not too late to come in for a cup of coffee, is it?' he suggested as he retrieved her bag from the back of the car.

'Oh, Matthew.' There was real regret in her voice as she hurried towards her front door. She would have loved to invite him in, to spend even a little more time with him, but it would only make it harder in the end.

'I'm so tired,' she murmured, 'and I've got a lot to do if I'm going to be straight in time to go back to work in the morning. I left the house in a bit of a mess when I went to work on Thursday.' She had her key ready in her hand and turned to face him as soon as she stepped inside the door.

'I'll see you at the hospital tomorrow, then,' she said brightly, holding out her hand for her bag.

'What's the matter, Hope?' Those laser-sharp eyes missed very little. 'Are you starting to feel guilty about going away with me? Is that why you're trying to—?'

'I didn't go away with you,' she objected pedantically. 'I didn't know you would be staying at the Manor too.'

'True,' he conceded. 'But I thought by the end of our stay you were quite pleased I was?'

Hope longed to agree, longed to throw caution and common sense to the winds and drag him inside her little house to continue where they'd left off, but she was too inexperienced to know if that was what he wanted. He'd been so silent on the return journey, after two days of talking about anything and everything under the sun. What other reason could there be than that he regretted their short-lived affair?

'Matthew, I can't talk now. I've got so much to do,' she protested weakly.

'All right, Hope.' He finally leant forward to deposit her bag at her feet and then straightened up swiftly to wrap her tightly in his arms, his lips taking hers in a mating every bit as passionate as those which had gone before. 'Sleep well, sweetheart. I'll see you in the morning.'

She shut the door quickly behind him but took the

half-dozen steps so that she could secretly watch him through the front window, standing back in the shadows so that he wouldn't know that she saw him getting into his car, her attention every bit as rapt as a teenager over a pop star.

'What on earth am I doing?' she muttered aloud as she watched him driving away. 'I'm a mature, adult woman, not some brainless twit mooning after a man because my hormones have just decided to wake up!'

She whirled away from the window and looked at the pristine neatness of the little room, regretting the lost chance to spend some more time with him. How much more would she regret it if it had been her *last* chance?

'No use crying over spilt milk,' she recited as she reached for the coffee-table in front of the settee and carried it to the far end of the room. 'If I keep myself busy I won't have time to notice he isn't here.' And she shifted the rest of the furniture aside so that she could begin to pin out the fabric for the wedding dresses.

She had backache the following morning as a result of spending too many hours crawling about on the floor, checking and rechecking her calculations and measurements before she finally set shears to fabric. A mistake at this stage could be extremely costly.

It was a rather daunting thought that she still had the same process to go over twice more with the bridesmaids' dresses, but she'd given her word and, in spite of her daughter's disparaging remarks, there would be nothing second best about these dresses.

It was a strangely unreal feeling to set foot inside

the ward the next morning. It was only two days since she'd last been on duty, but in some strange way it felt as if twenty years had gone by—as if the person who had left two days ago had been deep frozen inside by what had happened to her and the Sister Morgan who was just coming on duty was the woman she should have become years ago.

'Good morning, Sister,' Maggie called brightly. 'Mr Benedict's been up here looking for you.'

CHAPTER SEVEN

HOPE's heart leapt into her mouth. She'd expected at least a few minutes to get her nerves under control before she had to face her nemesis.

'Do you know what he wanted?' She concentrated on locking her purse away in the desk drawer, so that she wasn't looking directly at Maggie.

'He didn't say.' She shrugged. 'Just asked me to get you to contact him as soon as you arrived.' She looked over her shoulder towards the door like a character in a badly acted spy film. 'Have you had time to catch up on the gossip about him?' Her expression was avid.

'Who?' Hope blinked, her mind still occupied with trying to guess the reason why Matthew wanted to speak to her.

'Our Mr Benedict, that's who,' Maggie crowed. 'Honestly, Hope, sometimes I wonder if you've got any red blood in your veins.'

'What gossip?' Maggie's insult was too familiar to hurt.

'Well...' She settled one ample hip on the corner of the desk, as though she was making herself comfortable for a long session. 'You know that ever since he got here half the hospital have been setting their caps at him—well, the female half anyway.' She raised an eyebrow and chuckled at her own joke.

'Even Sexy Samantha up on Obs and Gobs gave it her best try, but he seemed to be immune. W-e-ll—'

she drew the word out into half a dozen syllables '—it seems as if he's fallen at last!' she finished on a triumphant note, and waited for Hope's reaction.

'Who?' She managed to force out the single word through suddenly dry lips.

'That's the tantalising part about it. No one knows who.'

'So how do they know there's anyone at all?' She held her breath as she waited for the proof that she'd been right all along—that someone like Matthew Benedict would only want a brief fling with the likes of Hope Morgan because he could choose from a whole string of women.

'Apparently he was seen escorting a stunning blonde into his car the other day, but the people who saw it happen either couldn't see her face or didn't recognise her.'

'Perhaps he was only giving someone a lift?' Hope suggested, more to ease her own disappointment in him than to give him an alibi.

'You wouldn't believe that if you'd seen him today,' Maggie gloated. 'The story is that he arranged a couple of days off for himself, and he's come back looking exhausted and with a smug grin all over his face!'

And the only person Matthew had been with for the last two days was. . .

With a sense of profound shock Hope suddenly realised that the 'stunning blonde' everyone was speculating about was herself!

She sat open-mouthed with amazement for several seconds before it dawned on her what a disaster it would be for their reputations if their time away together should ever become common knowledge.

'Well?' Maggie demanded impatiently. 'What do you think of that?'

'It seems as if a lot has been going on while I've been away,' Hope murmured noncommittally.

'Well, you certainly missed out on all the excitement,' Maggie agreed.

Hope resorted to biting the inside of her cheek when she realised that Maggie would kill her if she had any idea what had really gone on in the last two days.

'Hey, if you're going to see him in a minute, will you try to find out who she is?' Maggie's eyes were shining. 'A couple of nurses in Theatre have offered a reward for information leading to an identity.'

'You're mad, the lot of you,' Hope scolded, with fear in her heart. 'Obviously haven't got enough to do. . .'

Maggie slid to her feet and reversed rapidly towards the door with both hands held up in a placating way. 'I'm going. I'm going. Is that all the thanks I get for keeping you up to date with all the gossip. . .?'

Hope's hand hovered over the phone as soon as she was alone. Why had Matthew been trying to contact her? Had he heard the rumours going round and wanted to make sure she didn't put her foot in it—or get any false hopes?

The coward in Hope made her want to put off the evil hour as long as she could, but she knew that in a hospital it was impossible to ignore a request from a consultant to contact him. He might want to speak to her about the events of the last few days, but it could just as well be a life and death matter for a patient.

'Mr Benedict wanted to speak to me,' she informed his secretary as soon as they were connected. 'It's Sister Morgan on the paediatric ward.'

'I'm so sorry, Sister,' the pleasant voice apologised. 'I haven't got anything written down but he *was* called into Theatre in a hurry. Do you want me to get a message to him, or shall I get him to contact you when he comes out?'

'Oh. . .' Relief at her reprieve flooded through her. 'He can contact me when he's free,' Hope suggested, and put the phone down again.

She was on tenterhooks all day, with the prospect of talking to him hanging over her like the sword of Damocles. It wasn't as if she had time to spare either. Every bed on the ward was full, and she and her staff were kept constantly busy tending to one or another of their charges—almost falling over the legion of worried parents who were hovering over their sick children.

'Sister?' A tearful voice drew her attention to the doorway of her office.

'What's the matter, Laura?' She beckoned her in. 'Not having problems on your first day with us, are you?'

'I didn't realise how much difference there was between Paediatrics and other departments.' She slumped dejectedly into the chair Hope pointed out. 'At least with adult patients you can hold a conversation and reason with them, but most of that lot—' she indicated the patients on the other side of the observation window '—might just as well come from Mars for all the notice they take.'

Hope waited, sensing that she hadn't reached the end of her tale of woe. She was right.

'I was hoping to specialise in Paediatrics when I've

finished my training, but if this is what it's like I'm never going to make it!'

'So, what's gone wrong this morning to dump you in the depths of despair?'

'Staff Nurse asked me to take temperatures, but I can't get Tanis to open his mouth for me. Obviously I can't force him or he might bite it, but. . .' She shrugged and pulled an expressive face.

The little boy she was talking about was only in for observation after a bad fall, but as the child of a single parent he'd had to spend most of his stay without the reassuring presence of his mother, who couldn't afford to take time away from work.

'Have you got any brothers and sisters?' Hope probed, trying to find some way to help.

'No, I'm an only child.'

'What about pets?'

'Well, not really—I used to go horse riding, but how will that help?'

'I can remember someone once telling me that every girl ought to learn to ride a horse so that she learns early on in her life how to control something bigger and stupider than herself.'

Laura Nugent stared at Hope in surprise, then burst out laughing. 'I think I see your point,' she said, her face wreathed in a cheerful smile. 'Distract and conquer?'

'Exactly.' Hope nodded, pleased that she had read the girl's intelligence so accurately. 'Nursing children has its own frustrations, but I've always felt that it's the most rewarding side. Now, off you go and see what you come up with.'

Hope knew that she would be forgiven for eavesdropping on the young nurse's next attempt, especially if she could help her through her first day on the ward. She also knew that Laura's satisfaction would be far greater if she managed to solve the problem herself.

'Hello, Tanis.' Hope watched as the young nurse sat herself down beside the bed with a small boxful of items. The four-year-old looked at Laura with suspicion, his liquid chocolate eyes huge under a thick thatch of straight black hair. Hope couldn't help noticing that his little mouth was very firmly buttoned!

'Have you seen my teddy bear?' Laura took out one of the soft toys which were part of the basic equipment of a paediatric ward. 'He had a bad fall and hurt his head, so I'm going to put a bandage on him.'

Hope watched as the young woman started to apply a bandage to the bear's head. When her efforts kept sliding off, Hope was the only one to realise that it was deliberate. The little child was captivated by what she was doing, and couldn't wait to offer his assistance.

It was a matter of minutes before Tanis was guided into suggesting that the bear needed to have his temperature taken, and by then it was a foregone conclusion that he wouldn't be able to resist having his own taken for comparison.

'Well done, Laura,' Hope murmured softly as she watched the successful conclusion of the little game. 'I think we've got you well and truly hooked for a career in paediatric nursing!'

The busy ward routine continued, in spite of Hope's preoccupation with the telephone and the way her head turned instantly when she heard the sound of male footsteps entering the ward.

By the time she reached the end of her shift she was

exhausted, and only too ready to grab her belongings and make her way home. She would have loved to crawl straight into bed, but there was far too much sewing still to be done to allow her that luxury.

The various pieces of ivory silk which would eventually make the wedding dress had been left spread out flat on the carpet to prevent too much creasing, so it was important that she got the whole thing together before it got spoilt.

Several hours later there was a cup of coffee on the small table beside her chair that she'd left so long it had grown cold. She was just trying to decide whether to get up and make herself another when there was a sharp ring on the doorbell.

'Who on earth. . .?' She glanced up at the clock on the mantelpiece. 'It's gone ten o'clock. No one comes calling at this time of night. Unless. . .' She remembered her neighbour's distress at forgetting to deliver a parcel, and wondered if the same thing had happened again.

'If I don't get to the door soon, he's going to worry that he's got me out of bed, poor man,' she muttered as she extracted herself from the rustling sections of fabric and climbed carefully over the pieces still laid out flat. She was so worried that something might get spilt on it. . .

The bell rang a second time just as she was about to release the catch, and the echoes still surrounded her as she switched the porch light on and pulled the door open.

'Hope.'

Matthew stepped forward into the light and all the breath left her lungs in a rush.

When she'd left the hospital this afternoon she'd been relieved to think that she wouldn't have to confront him until tomorrow, but here he was.

'May I come in?' He tilted his head as he looked up at her, the step up to the front door giving her a slight height advantage. The light slanted across his face, highlighting the smooth planes of his forehead and cheeks and deepening the fan of tiny lines at the corners of his eyes.

He put one foot up on the step and she suddenly realised what he had said.

'No!' She gripped the edge of the door to prevent him coming in, horribly conscious of the precious fabric spread out on her floor. 'It's not a convenient time.'

'Not convenient?' His brows snapped together in a deep frown. 'I need to talk to you, Hope.'

'Can't it wait?' She ran her fingers through her dishevelled hair. 'I'll be seeing you at the hospital tomorrow. . .'

'Not if it's anything like today, you won't. Anyway—' he fixed her with a fierce stare '—it *won't* wait—*I* won't wait until tomorrow.' And he put the flat of one hand against the solid wood of her front door and pushed it out of her grasp.

'Matthew!' Hope had to step back quickly out of the path of the door, and was unable to prevent him stepping into her hallway and swinging the door shut behind him.

Before she could draw breath to demand an explanation for his caveman behaviour he'd reached out for her, and then she was wrapped tightly in his arms and his head was dipped towards her.

'*This* is what won't wait until tomorrow,' he breathed huskily as his lips met hers.

All thoughts of objecting vanished without trace as she opened her mouth for him the way he'd taught her to, the way she loved to welcome him into her body, to tease and taunt until he couldn't wait to replace the imitation of lovemaking with the real thing.

'Oh, God, Hope, I've missed you,' he murmured as he strung kisses over her face and down the curve of her neck. 'I've been trying to get up to the ward to see you all day, but they've had me dashing about. . .' He lost his train of thought—or she did—as his hands cupped the softness of her breasts through her clothing and feathered over the tell-tale nipples.

'I need you,' he groaned as he reached for the hem of her lightweight jumper and stripped it over her head in a single movement. 'Oh, Hope, I need you.' And he slipped the silky straps of her bra off her shoulders to release her smooth warmth into his waiting palms.

'Please.' The word was hardly more than a breath as she arched her back towards him and linked her fingers in the thickness of the silky hair at the back of his head, but he heard it and knew what she wanted.

'Like this?' he teased as he lapped at her rosy crests like a kitten tasting milk. 'Or like *this*?' And he opened his mouth to suckle her until the strength disappeared from her legs and she sank against him with a cry.

The powerful arms which bound her to his body were the only reason why she remained upright, her whole body trembling with arousal.

'Hope?' His husky use of her name was a demand that she was helpless to refuse.

'Oh, Matthew.' She wrapped her arms tightly around

his shoulders as he lifted her and turned to pin her against the solid wood of the front door. 'Here?' she squeaked in surprise. 'Like this?'

'Here,' he growled as he slid both hands up her thighs, taking her skirt with them until their whole slender length was bared to his touch.

One hand was enough to strip her silky panties away from underneath her skirt, but the other one joined it to caress the sweet roundness of her hips and thighs.

'Now,' he groaned deeply. 'Ah, sweetheart, now.' And seconds later he cried out as he joined their bodies together, her legs wrapped tightly around him as he took them both to heaven.

'Matthew?' Hope murmured when she finally found enough breath to speak.

'Mmm?' he growled huskily against her throat, his body still pinning her against her front door.

'Why?' Hope could feel the heat rising in her face as she tried to visualise what they looked like.

'Why what?' he mumbled, as if he was bereft of strength.

'Why here...like this?' She could hear the confusion in her own voice.

There were several seconds of silence before he lifted his head and their eyes met. 'You want the truth?' he questioned.

'Yes.' She nodded, suddenly aware of the colour rising up his throat and across his cheekbones.

'Because I couldn't wait any longer,' he said simply as he let her see the honest passion in his eyes.

Hope was stunned. Nothing like this had ever happened to her before; no one had ever looked at her with desire so she hadn't known...

'Is it always like this for you?' she asked in a very small voice, her eyes flitting shyly away from direct contact with his.

'Never.' He was adamant, his hand cupping her cheek and bringing her face back to his until she met his gaze again. 'It *never* been like this for me before.' And he tilted his head to kiss her lips in sweet benediction.

It was some time later that Matthew was sitting in the kitchen cradling a cup of coffee after he'd finished the omelette Hope had made for him.

He was gazing pensively into the last few mouthfuls in the bottom of the cup, and Hope guessed that he was steeling himself to speak.

She wrapped her arms around herself, hugging the warmth of the towelling dressing gown she'd donned after the shower they'd shared until the water had grown cold...

'Hope?' He finally looked up from his contemplation. 'Why did you try to stop me coming in? Why didn't you want me in your home?'

'Oh, Matthew.' Her voice was filled with relief. If that was all that was worrying him...'Come with me and I'll show you.' She stood up and held out her hand, shivering deliciously when he laced his fingers through hers.

'That's why.' She pushed the sitting room door open just far enough for him to see the yards of ivory silk lying in billows across the floor. 'I'm terrified of something happening to it before it's finished and covered in plastic.'

'It's a beautiful fabric.' He wrapped an arm around

her shoulders and pulled her to lean against him. 'Are you enjoying making the dress?'

'Yes and no,' Hope admitted. 'It's a big responsibility, because she'll be the focus of all eyes on the day, and I'm dreading Jane coming down at the weekend.'

'Have you had words?'

'Hardly. She hasn't bothered to contact me at all.' Hope tilted her chin up, as if her daughter's thoughtlessness didn't matter. 'Actually, it's fitting the dress that's worrying me most at the moment. I've had to redraft a commercial pattern to her specifications, but when I looked at the style she'd chosen it had a great gaping V back and front, and the body of the dress was designed to be skin-tight right to her hips.'

'And?' He leant his head forward until his cheek was resting on her hair, his body propped comfortably against the doorframe. 'I take it you've made some changes?'

'Well, apart from completely redesigning the sleeves she didn't like, the neckline has come up at the front and the back, and the line of the bodice now tapers out from just below the waist until it forms a short train at the hem, so it only hints at the body underneath instead of revealing it. . .'

'Why did you make the extra changes?' There was open curiosity in his voice.

'Because. . . Well, the style was far more suitable for a sophisticated evening dress, not a wedding dress to be worn in a church while a marriage is being solemnised. It just doesn't seem like the right place to flaunt a young woman's assets with yards of bare flesh. If it had just been a register office. . .' She shrugged.

'So you're dreading Jane coming down because you

think she'll object to the way you've changed the design?'

'Maybe.' She shrugged again. 'It's easy enough to take the seams in again until it fits her like a sausage skin, and lowering the neckline only takes a few minutes, but I'm hoping that when she sees herself in the dress she'll love the way it looks on her too much to want to change it.'

She sighed tiredly. 'For the first time in her life, I really can't say I'm looking forward to seeing her, and it makes me feel very sad...'

They stood in silence, his arms cradling her against his body as they looked at the trappings of her daughter's new life, and she suddenly felt very old.

'Where does time go?' she murmured as she reached out to pull the door closed. 'One minute I was eighteen, with my whole life ahead of me, and the next time I looked it was all behind me...'

'Your life is a long way from over, sweetheart.' His deep voice was a verbal caress, but she was too tired to respond—too cold in the quiet places inside for his warmth to penetrate.

'I must go to bed, Matthew. I'd never forgive myself if I couldn't do my job properly because I was too tired.' She raised blue-grey eyes to travel over his familiar features, using the tip of one finger to trace the line of his eyebrow down to the curve of his cheekbone until she reached the corner of his mouth.

'Goodnight, sweetheart.' He captured her wrist in his hand and kissed the fingertip before he touched it to her own mouth. 'See you tomorrow,' he murmured, and let himself quietly out of the front door.

* * *

The sound of a child in distress was the first thing Hope heard when she opened the door to the ward the next morning.

'Good morning, Sister.' Matthew's grey-green eyes sent secret messages of welcome while he introduced her to their new patient.

'This is Amy Harper and she's five years old.' He smiled gently at the tearstained youngster curled up on her mother's lap. 'Her parents took her to their GP with a high temperature. She wasn't eating well, was wanting to be carried everywhere and was complaining that her hip hurt.'

'Our doctor saw her about two weeks ago, after she'd had a fall at school,' Mrs Harper explained. 'She had a terrible bruise on her hip but it seemed to get better. Now she's complaining that the pain has come back, and it's very hot and red.' There was a worried look on her face as she stroked the silky russet hair away from her daughter's hot forehead.

'Sister Scott took blood and sent the sample up to the lab before she went off duty. Amy will be going across to Radiology for X-rays in a minute,' Matthew detailed. 'In the meantime, we need to get her on some fairly hefty pain relief as soon as possible and get her comfortable while we wait for the lab results.'

It was a difficult job getting Amy settled. Her parents were so worried about their only child that they were trying to overprotect her, and this was getting her even more worked up.

In the end Hope resorted to sending them off one at a time on helpful errands, so that she and the child only had one parent to contend with.

Once the painkillers were doing their work the little

girl was quieter and calmer, and this seemed to help the parents to relax.

Unfortunately, when the lab had finished their tests, Hope had to call Matthew back up to the ward to explain the bad news to the Harpers.

'When Amy fell, she damaged the top of her leg bone, close to the hip,' he began, carefully avoiding the frightening use of long Latin words. 'An infection has started in the bone and she'll need several weeks of treatment with antibiotics to make sure that we get rid of it.'

'How many tablets will she have to take, Mr Benedict? Only, she's not very good at swallowing them.'

'Initially the drugs will be given in hospital, because they have to be given intravenously and it's important that we keep the right level in the blood. She'll also have what we call a back-slab of plaster of Paris to immobilise her leg, because that will help to reduce the pain.'

'How badly is this infection going to affect her leg?' Mr Harper was looking quite green. 'Will it spread to the rest of her body if you don't treat it?'

'From the tests and the pictures we took it looks as if you brought her to your doctor when the infection was just getting started, so there's a good chance that she'll recover well. Osteomyelitis isn't the sort of infection that can get better on its own, and it can be a fairly long job getting rid of it.'

'How long will she have to be in hospital? Only, she was doing really well in school. . .'

'I shouldn't worry about that, Mrs Harper.' Hope stepped into the conversation. 'We have a teacher who comes in to the ward to help the children to keep up with their schoolwork. If you have a word with Amy's teacher about the work she should be covering, between us we can make sure that she doesn't miss out.'

'Are there any other questions you'd like to ask?' Matthew looked from one to the other as they shook their heads. 'You're probably shell-shocked at the moment, but when your brains start working you can always ask Sister if there's anything you don't understand.'

'And if I can't tell you the answer, Mr Benedict is always coming down to the ward to check on the patients,' Hope added. 'In the meantime, I can see that Amy's dozing now that the pain's been taken away, so I suggest that the two of you go exploring together to learn your way around the hospital—it helps if you don't get lost every time you come in!'

'There's also a cafeteria, where you can get everything from a cup of coffee to a hot meal.' Matthew smiled. 'I suggest that the two of you take yourselves for a quiet sit down and a chat. You're going to be a very important part of Amy's recovery, so you've got to get your emotions under control or you won't be any help to her.'

The Harpers went to have a look at their daughter, to reassure themselves that she was resting calmly, then left the ward, letting Hope know that they would be back in an hour if Amy was to waken and fret for them.

'How much damage showed up on the X-rays?' Hope asked once they were out of earshot.

'Bearing in mind that at her age the progress of the disease wouldn't be seen for at least five days, there's very little evidence of inflammation and none at all of degeneration—so far.'

'So you'll be able to use those plates as a basis for comparison as treatment progresses,' Hope confirmed.

'Exactly.' Matthew nodded and glanced at the case-notes. 'Can you get someone to special her until we're certain that IV is running fast enough? She's quite small and we might have to switch needle sites or do a venous cutdown to increase the rate of flow.'

'I'll also get her monitored for drug reaction,' Hope proposed. 'Her parents said she'd never had antibiotics before, but we might end up having to give her a cocktail of them, so it's as well to be on the look-out.'

'Any other problems for me to look at while I'm here?' Matthew handed the notes back for filing and glanced down at his watch. 'If not, I've got time to drink a quick cup of coffee with you and raid your biscuit tin.'

Hope was well aware that his suggestion was part of his usual routine, and that none of the staff listening to their conversation would hear anything amiss—but *they* weren't seeing the wicked gleam in his eye when he mentioned raiding her biscuit tin, and she alone knew that it had been put there by the thought of spending time with her rather than the thought of chocolate digestives.

'Aren't you due in Theatre soon?' Hope checked the time on her own fob-watch. 'You can't expect some poor patient to lie there waiting for you to turn up while you sit eating me out of house and home!'

With her office door open and the observation window taking up most of one wall it was impracticable for them to do anything other than talk, but the atmosphere between them was alive with unspoken thoughts and desires and the potent memories of what had gone before.

In spite of that, they each seemed to find fresh energy for the tasks ahead with nothing more intimate to sustain them than social conversation with each other, and no closer contact than the accidental brush of fingers as a cup was offered and accepted.

Even the sudden electronic bleep of Matthew's pager couldn't spoil their time together, and his hasty, 'I'll call,' before he took off towards the accident department left Hope with a happy warmth around her heart.

Hope should have known that life was sailing along far too smoothly.

For nearly a week the ward had functioned with no more than the usual highs and lows in the treatment of their various young charges, and her work on the wedding dresses had progressed far faster than she had expected.

She and Matthew had even managed to snatch a few hours together at odd intervals—once to go out for a meal, another time to go for a long walk on a perfect afternoon.

More often than not they elected to spend time quietly together—Matthew taking over the cooking while Hope got on with the sewing.

Each time he looked at his watch and stood up to go, Hope wished she had the courage to ask him to stay. She longed to wake up in the morning and see his head on the pillow beside her as she had at the Manor, but she couldn't bring herself to take the final step.

She told herself that it was because Jane was coming home at the weekend to have her dress fitted, but deep inside she knew that it was her own uncertainty which was making her hesitate.

It had taken many hours of gazing up at a darkened ceiling before she had finally admitted that she'd cut herself off from other people for so long that she didn't trust her own judgement, and she was clinging to the part-time affair she had with Matthew instead of taking a chance on a committed relationship.

'My daughter's got more courage than I have,' she scolded herself as she put fresh sheets on Jane's bed on Thursday. 'At least she and Edward are jumping in at the deep end... I'm just paddling my toes in the shallow water.'

She stood back and looked around to see if everything was ready. This was the larger of the two bedrooms and had been Jane's room ever since the two of them had moved there. It was still full of her belongings, and Hope couldn't help wondering what it would look like once she took the mementoes off the walls and the ornaments off the shelves.

Suddenly it dawned on Hope that in a very few weeks this room would be permanently empty, and she realised that there was no reason why she shouldn't move herself out of the tiny box bedroom into this much bigger room.

'I could leave all my sewing things where they are,' she muttered as she stood in the doorway of her own room and looked at the shelves full of clutter. 'This could be my sewing room, and if I move my bed into her room and replace her bed with a couch that visitors can use...'

At first Matthew laughed at her excitement over her plans to reorganise, but when they were curled up together later that evening he told her that he understood her reasons.

'It's a bit like a bereavement, I suppose,' he mused into her rumpled curls. 'Your relationship with Jane has changed and she'll never be coming back here to live, so you have to reclaim her territory for your own.'

'Exactly.' Hope reached up to press a grateful kiss to his roughened chin. 'Apart from the fact that it's a much bigger room and I'll be able to fit a full-sized double bed in there.' She drew a sharp breath as she heard the words which had escaped from her mouth, suddenly realising that it was tantamount to suggesting that she wanted his approval for her plans, that she wanted to know if she was going to be sharing the bed with him.

'But I rather like your cosy bed.' His voice rumbled around in his chest as she pressed her ear over his heart, and for a moment she wasn't certain what he meant.

'On the other hand—' he rolled over suddenly, catching her unawares '—a bigger bed would mean more space to play.' And she was pinned helplessly underneath him as he started to tickle her.

CHAPTER EIGHT

'I'VE brought Liz and Anne with me,' Jane announced as Hope opened the door to her on Friday night. 'I thought it would be easier if we got it all over in one go.'

Hope had heard Jane's car arrive and had been eager to welcome her home, longing to heal the rift which had opened up between them. Now her heart was sinking as the three of them trooped in and dumped various items of luggage in a pile in her tiny hall. With Liz and Anne here there would be little chance for the two of them to talk—a fact which Jane was probably counting on.

'What about beds?' Hope murmured weakly as Jane led the way into the kitchen and began to raid the fridge.

'No problem.' Jane waved a purloined chicken leg airily. 'These two have brought sleeping bags. All you need to find are pillows.' And she reached out to switch the kettle on. 'Tea or coffee?' she offered the room at large.

It was an hour before any of them were ready to get down to the purpose of the visit, and Hope was left feeling frustrated by her inability to get them to stand still long enough for her to do an accurate job first time. She was glad, now, that she had spent so much time on the accuracy of her preparations, because—luckily—the fit of all three dresses was very good.

After her careful concern for the precious fabric she was terrified of working on Jane's ivory dress while the three of them wandered around with coffee-cups in their hands, and she ended up taking it up to her room to work on it alone.

She stayed working until long after midnight, listening to the muffled sound of the television drifting up from the sitting room as the three of them watched a late-night film.

A perfectionist by nature, she was painstakingly inserting the long zips in the dresses by hand, so that they wouldn't show in any of the photos, and was determined that she would finish all three before she went to bed.

She was up again early in the morning to set the sleeves in and pin the hems ready for the next fitting, then had to twiddle her thumbs while she waited for them to surface from Jane's room.

By the time the three of them were ready to leave on the Sunday afternoon Hope felt as if she'd been run over by a bus—twice!

Jane had decided on the Saturday evening that she wanted to have a hand in the making of her dress, and had sat for several hours hand-sewing her way round the yards and yards of hem while her friends had kept her company with whispers and gales of giggles overlaid by awful loud music.

The bridesmaids' dresses still needed their hems finished, but as Liz and Anne hadn't bought their shoes yet Jane had volunteered to do them herself, later.

'We don't want to have to come all the way back down here again,' she'd laughed. 'Now that we've done most of it, I can finish the rest off in no time. It will leave you more time to make a good job of the cake.' And the dresses had been wrapped in dustbin bags and haphazardly bundled into the car with the rest of the luggage and they had waved goodbye.

As if he knew that she was standing just inside the door surveying the chaos, the telephone rang and there was Matthew's voice in her ear.

'Are they still there or is it safe to come round?' he demanded gruffly.

'They've just gone, but the whole house looks as if a bomb exploded in it.' Hope gazed round, absent-mindedly counting the number of cups left standing on tables, windowsills and the carpet—and that was just in the sitting room.

'Shall I come round and cook you something?' he offered. 'You sound frazzled.'

'I am,' Hope admitted. 'But you can't cook anything because there isn't anything left to cook. Those three were like a plague of locusts.'

'I'll bring something with me,' he promised. 'Don't bother to tidy up. Just sit down and put your feet up and I'll be there as soon as I can.'

Hope had gathered up the dirty cups and the sitting room was looking reasonably tidy by the time she heard his car draw up outside the house.

She was on her way through to the kitchen with the last handful of dirty crockery, and detoured to open the door for him on her way towards the bowl full of hot soapy water.

'I told you to leave it, you stubborn woman,' he grumbled as he followed her, his hands busy juggling the familiar packages of a take-away meal.

'As you can see, I haven't begun to sort this room out.' Hope wrinkled her nose at the piles of pots and pans and dirty plates. 'If it had just been Jane, I would have reminded her to clear up after herself, but it's more difficult when she brings unexpected guests with her.'

'Did you have any time to talk?' He reached up to the cupboard where her plates lived with an easy familiarity that warmed Hope's heart, only to mutter imprecations when he found that there were none left.

'Grab a teatowel and I'll wash a couple.' Hope slid her hands into the suds and found two plates.

'You're supposed to be putting your feet up,' he complained as she whisked the bubbles off under running water. 'You probably need another holiday after this marathon.'

'I'm just grateful I don't have to cook this evening.' She reached up to press a kiss to his cheek, relishing the rasp of the emerging stubble and breathing in the smell of herbs and musk which seemed a part of his skin.

'Well...' The two plates dried, he deposited the cloth beside the draining board. 'You've got five minutes to do whatever you need to do—dry your hands, wash your face or whatever—then your meal will be ready to eat.' He grabbed the carrier bags and plates and left the kitchen on the way to the sitting room.

Their time soaking in the hot water made the cups and plates easy to clean, and within the allotted time she had a neat pile of washing-up draining beside the sink and was rubbing cream into her hands. The comb and lipstick in her bag took care of the essential neatening process, and she left the kitchen to join Matthew with a lighter step than she could ever have thought possible just half an hour ago.

'Matthew...!' She paused in the doorway to the

sitting room to take in the transformation. 'How did you manage all this?'

The coffee-table was drawn up in front of the settee, a lighted candle at each end setting off gleams around the edges of the plates and wineglasses he'd laid out.

'If madam would like to take a seat?' He held out one hand and bowed as obsequiously as any head waiter. 'Dinner is served.'

'Matthew, you're an idiot.' She couldn't help the delighted smile which crept over her face. 'But a nice idiot.'

'In which case, I think I'll collect the kiss I didn't get when I arrived,' he murmured as he wrapped her in his arms.

Their lips had hardly met when someone's stomach rumbled, and they both burst out laughing.

'It's the smell of the food that does it,' Hope said as she settled herself in front of the table and peered under each of the lids. 'Oh, good. Chicken and beansprouts...and prawns... I'm ravenous!'

For the next fifteen minutes the only conversation was about the food, and it wasn't until Hope groaned and leant back against the settee that Matthew refilled her glass and handed it to her.

He picked up his own wine, his elbows planted on his thighs as he hunched forward to gaze at the straw-coloured liquid.

'I've missed you the last couple of days,' he said into the easy silence which had fallen between them, and turned to gaze into her eyes.

'I missed you too,' Hope admitted, her tongue loosened by tiredness and the unaccustomed wine. 'I had a houseful of noisy young women and I was so busy I hardly had time to draw breath but I was lonely.'

'Ah, Hope—' he gave a lopsided smile '—so straightforward and honest.' He reached out one hand to grasp hers, his gaze growing suddenly intense. 'Perhaps that's why I've fallen in love with you. . .'

'You. . .?' Hope gasped with shock. Of all the things he could have said, she would never have expected this.

'I'm sorry. Perhaps I shouldn't have said anything so soon, but when you said you'd missed me too I couldn't help—'

'I love you too,' she blurted out, her heart trying to beat its way out of her throat. 'Oh, Matthew, I do.' And emotional tears trickled from each eye as he gently removed the glass still clutched tightly in her hand and set it on the table beside his before taking her in his arms.

It was enough for Hope just to be held, her head resting on his shoulder while he drew her against the powerful protection of his body, but eventually the rosy mists began to clear.

'What are we going to do about it?' she asked in a small voice, her brain running in circles around the fact that they worked together at the hospital and that Jane and Edward were getting married in a matter of weeks.

'I realise I'm no one's idea of a prize.' He shrugged. 'I suppose I'm too set in my ways as a crusty bachelor, and too long in the tooth for anyone to want to take me on. . .'

Hope was distracted. At first she thought that he was joking, but then she realised that he actually believed what he was saying, and she marvelled at the fact that he honestly hadn't realised that half the female staff at

St Augustine's had been trying to get their hooks into him for the past year.

'Will you give me a chance?' he said insistently as he cradled her face with one hand. 'Can we see if we can make anything of it?'

'It depends what...what you're thinking of,' she stammered, certain that while she was coming to terms with his guileless self-image she must have missed something. He couldn't mean...

'I want us to get married,' he said firmly. 'I don't like this business of having to steal time away from our other commitments to be with each other.'

'You mean, because of the fact that we both work at the hospital?' Was it only propriety that was making him take such a step?

'No, dammit! I mean because I don't like wasting precious time travelling backwards and forwards between your place and mine when we could be spending that time together. I mean because I don't like waking up alone when I know what it's like to wake up beside you.'

'Oh, Matthew, I know what you're saying because I feel the same way. I hate having to watch you drive away at the end of an evening.' She smiled tremulously, then sighed. 'But what about Jane and Edward? How would we—?'

'I have no desire to wake up beside Jane and Edward,' he joked indignantly, then he became very serious. 'Their relationship has nothing whatever to do with ours apart from the fact that it was instrumental in getting us together,' he declared.

'But...'

'But nothing,' he said firmly. 'The first time I met

you, a year ago at that awful "meet the consultant" party, I was knocked out by you, but I couldn't do anything about it because I thought you were married.'

'You glared at me as if I was something nasty you'd found under your shoe,' Hope reminded him.

'I overheard what Maggie Philp said to you, and it sounded as if you were the sort of woman who wasn't particularly bothered about being faithful to your vows. It wasn't until much later that I found out that you weren't married any longer.'

'But because you thought I played the field you still weren't interested?'

'Oh, I was still interested—very interested.' His eyes moved over her face hotly. 'But I've never been one to take part in those sophisticated games of musical chairs.'

'Me? Sophisticated?' Hope chuckled. 'Was it a terrible let-down when you realised that I was more a hot cocoa person than a champagne and caviare one?'

'No. Relieved.' He smiled ruefully. 'I've never had much of a taste for extravagance for its own sake.'

'But. . .' She bit her lip.

'What?'

'Well. . .it's about Edward and the wedding.' Suddenly she wished she'd kept quiet. Why had she had to bring that topic into the conversation? The last thing she wanted to do was insult him on their special evening, but after hearing his views about unnecessary extravagance she was puzzled.

'Jane has never been brought up to have extravagant tastes because we've never had the money,' she said by way of preamble. 'So when she started telling me about the expensive wedding they were planning I thought it must be because Edward was accustomed to such things.'

She watched as an unexpected tide of embarrassment coloured his cheekbones.

'That's probably my fault,' he admitted. 'When he lost both his parents like that I suppose I tended to overcompensate.'

'And it doesn't take long before children realise which side their bread is buttered.' Hope nodded her quick understanding. 'It's just a shame that their pride has forced them into spending so much on empty trappings.'

'What do you mean?'

'Well, I was perfectly willing to give Jane the wedding myself, but when she phoned up to inform me of their plans and demand a cheque for the deposit I had to tell her that it was well beyond my means, and she went off in a huff.'

The memory of Jane's hurtful taunt that Hope was always satisfied with second best still rankled.

'When she finally got back to me, she said that she and Edward had done some thinking and had decided to foot the bill themselves.'

Matthew gave a strangled gasp, and Hope twisted to look up at him.

'That's what she told you?' he said gruffly, a strange expression crossing his face.

'Yes.' Hope smiled. 'Of course, I was still upset that they'd cut me out without even coming down to discuss it with me, but on the other hand I was really proud of them for being so determined about what they wanted and for their willingness to shoulder the cost themselves.'

Matthew's strange stillness finally registered with Hope, and she looked at him carefully.

'Matthew? What's wrong?'

'Oh, Hope.' He sighed and shook his head, his hands coming up to grasp her shoulders and lift her away from her comfortable niche against his body.

Hope sat up, a cold chill of premonition travelling the length of her spine as Matthew rose to his feet and put his hands in his pockets. The ridges of his knuckles outlined against the fabric of his trousers told her that they had been clenched into tight fists.

'She didn't tell you the truth,' he said quietly as he drew his hands out again, letting them hang by his sides as he squared his shoulders like a man about to face a firing squad.

'Didn't. . .?' Hope gazed up at him in confusion. 'What truth?'

'That they asked me to pay for the wedding.'

His words were a blow every bit as violent as a physical one, and Hope felt sick at the impact.

'You?' she whispered as betrayal surged through her in an acid flood. 'You've been going behind my back all this time?'

'No, Hope.' He denied the accusation vehemently. 'They told me that you. . .' But she wasn't listening. She couldn't hear anything above the roaring in her ears.

Jane had lied again, she thought, and bile rose up in her throat. It seemed as if that was all her daughter had been doing ever since she'd gone away to college, as if she'd completely forgotten the saying Hope had taught her to live by—tell the truth and shame the devil. Except that Jane was the one shamed now, damned out of her own mouth by lie after lie.

'How could you?' she choked, lifting tear-filled eyes towards him. In the romantic candlelight he almost seemed to shimmer like a mirage, an imitation of the man she had thought he was. 'How long were you going to keep the deception up? Until after the wedding?'

'Hope, I didn't know she hadn't told you. I had no idea that they were saying different things to each of us...'

A thought suddenly struck her, and she continued as though he hadn't spoken.

'How many other lies are there?' she demanded frantically. 'Have I been wasting my time making cakes and dresses? Am I going to arrive at the church to find you've paid for a top designer model so she doesn't have to get married in second best? Will there be a professionally decorated cake waiting at the reception?'

'No, Hope,' he said intently as he paced backwards and forwards in front of the empty fireplace like a caged tiger. 'You must know that I wouldn't do something like that.'

The pain was growing like a cancer metastasising at the speed of light until it filled her, blinding her to the pain in his eyes and the desperation in his voice.

'What about this?' She gestured towards the remains of their meal, her throat hoarse with the effort to contain the tears as her heart shattered. 'Was this all a lie too?'

Sudden fury lent strength to her legs and she surged out of the settee.

'I want you to go, Matthew.' She spoke through gritted teeth as she stalked towards the door, a ghastly chasm opening up inside her.

'No, Hope. Not until we've talked...'

'Talked?' There was incredulity in her voice as she swung round to glare at him. 'I thought we'd been talking for weeks, but obviously the word means different things to the two of us. Please go away.' She bit the inside of her lip hard enough to draw blood in her effort to stay in control.

'But I love you,' he said hoarsely. 'Doesn't that mean anything to you?'

'It would if I could trust you to tell the truth, but I can't, can I?' She reached for the catch and swung the front door open, holding it in front of herself like a shield, and stared coldly at him as he retrieved his jacket and slung it over one shoulder.

'Hope.' He held one hand out in appeal as he made a last attempt to speak to her. 'Please, don't let the children come between us. It's all just a silly misunderstanding.'

'Hardly a misunderstanding,' she snapped. 'You knew how I felt about the wedding right from the first. The two of them would never have come to you behind my back if they hadn't thought you would go against me...' She shook her head as her throat closed up completely.

He stepped towards her, concern in his darkened eyes, but she waved him away, knowing that she wouldn't be able to bear it if he touched her.

'Just go,' she whispered, turning her head away to gaze out into the darkness.

It was hard going into work the next morning. Knowing that she would be seeing Matthew at intervals throughout the day made it so much more difficult to come to terms with the extremes of emotion she had suffered in the space of just a few hours.

Somehow, because she still loved her daughter, she could find it in her heart to excuse Jane's behaviour on the grounds of immaturity and selfish arrogance. Hopefully, the passage of time would cure her of both, and she would eventually become more adult.

The pain that cut deepest was Matthew's duplicity in agreeing to foot the bill for their pretentious excesses without first checking with her. Surely he had come to know a little about her in all the time they'd been spending together, otherwise why would he have proposed marriage last night?

Swiftly she slammed the door shut on that memory. She wasn't ready to cope with the pain of losing what she had only just found, and decided that the only way to stop herself from thinking about it was to immerse herself in work.

'Three for Theatre this morning,' Doris detailed as she handed over the ward to Hope's care. 'The first one's Mark MacDowell. He's four and he's going up for the final stage of his facial surgery. Mr Benedict will be assisting Mr Shaunessy from Maxillofacial.'

Hope glanced across at the child they were talking about and saw that he was happily sitting up and chatting with his far drowsier neighbour, almost ignoring his parents.

She'd seen the clinical photographs taken when he was born with a severe hare lip and cleft palate, and she could hardly believe that this was the same child.

The second photos in the file had been taken after the first operation, when he had been just hours old, and the improvement in his physical appearance after his lip had been repaired was amazing. The second operation at four months had repaired the roof of his mouth, so that there was less likelihood of damage to his speech and hearing and to make eating easier.

This final stage, now that he was four, would hopefully be the last time he needed to come into hospital, and it entailed inserting cartilage into his nose to correct his profile.

'Sister!' His chirpy voice hailed her across the ward as he caught sight of her. 'I'm here!'

'Hello, Mark. I can see you.' She went across to him, drawn by his happy exuberance. 'Mr and Mrs MacDowell.' She smiled. 'No point in asking how he's feeling about all this?'

'I'm amazed,' said his father in his distinctive Scots accent. 'We know he doesn't remember his first two operations because he was so young, but when the surgeon suggested we brought him to have a look at the ward to help him get used to the idea we hardly expected him to view it as a holiday!'

'He won't be feeling quite so chirpy after the operation, but it makes such a difference if they start off with a good attitude.' She pulled a slight face. 'I always feel so sorry for the little ones who've been fed on a diet of horror stories by older children before they get here.'

'The other child—' Mrs MacDowell glanced towards the next bed '—seems much sleepier than Mark.'

'To a certain extent that can depend on the individual child, but sometimes it's because they're on other medication at the same time as their pre-med.'

'We were beginning to wonder if you were going to

have to use a rubber mallet to knock him out!' his father teased.

'I think we'll manage without resorting to that!' Hope grinned. 'We always have so far...'

The sound of the double ward doors being opened drew everyone's attention as the porters appeared.

'Who's first for a ride?' the younger one asked Hope as he mimed pushing up his sleeves for a heavy job.

'Me! Me!' Mark squealed, and bounced on the bed.

'Is that right, Sister?' He shook his head, then scratched it. 'I think he's got so much energy that we'll sit on the bed and he can push us!'

Hope left them arguing the toss quite happily while she checked the paperwork which was to travel down with Mark.

She carefully matched the details on his wristbands with his case-notes and handed them over to Polly Turner, who was to accompany him all the way from the ward to the theatre complex, where the hand-over to Theatre staff would happen.

After that, it was up to Mr Shaunessy and Matthew...

Just the thought of his name was like drawing sandpaper over an open wound, so she blocked him out, trying to relegate him to his old iceman persona.

It didn't work for long.

If his name wasn't being mentioned by one of the staff or the parents he was there in person, making his usual check to see how his patients were faring.

'Well, Mr and Mrs MacDowell.' He smiled, but Hope could see that he was tired, the muscles around his eyes tense. 'We were very pleased with how the operation went. He'll obviously be swollen and sore for the next few days, but after that he'll be back to his usual bouncy self.'

'You didn't find a volume control in there while you were operating?' his father joked.

'Sorry.' Matthew shook his head. 'You'll just have to make the best of the next few hours!'

Hope found herself chuckling, too, enjoying the lighter-hearted moments in a place which saw too much tragedy.

Unfortunately, the fact that he'd shown himself to be untrustworthy towards her on a personal level didn't detract in any way from her admiration of Matthew as a paediatrician. He was a superb clinical and surgical technician, and his patients and their families loved him...

So do I, the little voice of honesty spoke up inside her head. I still love him so much that now I can't be with him any more I feel as if I'm only half alive.

CHAPTER NINE

'WHEN is she coming in?'

Hope tucked the telephone receiver between her chin and her shoulder while she tapped into the computer to access the records she needed. She gave a silent sigh of relief as the right details came up on the screen—she wasn't very confident with the new system, and it had been known for her to have to make several attempts.

Ben Overton had even gone so far as to suggest that the children on the ward would probably be able to make a better job of the computer technology than Hope did.

'That's Alice Mary Harrison?' she confirmed, her eyes travelling swiftly over the details. 'She'll be with us in about half an hour?'

At the sound of footsteps she turned in time to see Matthew arrive at her doorway. As ever, her concentration faltered, and she almost forgot the poor person on the other end of the phone.

'Are you here about Alice Harrison?' she spoke while she was returning the receiver, so that she could look away from him and break the spell. In four weeks it hadn't got any easier. . .

'We've been hanging on as long as we can because of her other problems, but she's been having repeated chest infections and her GP is convinced she can't take any more.'

'When will she have surgery?'

'As soon as she's stable enough.' He scowled. 'She's had a rough six months, poor kid.'

Hope glanced back down at the information.

'As if she didn't have enough problems being born with Down's syndrome, she's also ended up with a fairly large hole in her heart.'

'Unfortunately, ventricular septal defect is associated with about thirty-five percent of Down's children, and they're also prone to acute leukaemia. So far Alice has escaped that complication...'

'What tests do you want done and how soon?' Briskness was her only defence against the attraction she still felt towards him.

'Can you organise a chest X-ray and electrocardiogram as soon as we get her settled here? We'll probably also need to do a fairly rapid cardiac catheterisation so we can plan the surgery...'

The sound of the doors opening heralded the arrival of the patient they were discussing, and Hope was immediately worried by how ill she looked.

For all that she was trying so hard to look at everything around her, and smile at each person she passed, her face was pale and sweaty and her breathing was far too fast.

'Hello, sweetheart,' Matthew murmured as he returned her smile, and Hope's heart dived towards her sensible shoes when she remembered that he had once called *her* his sweetheart.

She needed to get away for a few seconds, and beckoned Maggie across.

'We'll probably need to connect into the piped oxygen supply as soon as she's in bed, and she'll need to be propped up at forty-five degrees to help her breathing. If we support her arms on pillows it'll lessen the load on her heart.'

Maggie hurried off to sort out the equipment they needed and Hope returned her attention to Matthew's conversation with Alice's parents.

'Your doctor was quite right to send you in with her,' he was confirming reassuringly. 'She's having to fight far too hard, and it can only be causing more problems.'

'Will you be able to operate?' Mrs Harrison cradled the placid child against her shoulder. 'When she was diagnosed we were told that she'd have to wait until she was a year old.'

'Some heart defects like the one Alice has will actually repair themselves—depending on the severity. With the others, if we can possibly leave the children until they're a little bigger we stand a better chance of success.'

'Does that mean Alice doesn't stand a chance?' Mr Harrison demanded. 'She's our only child, and although it was a terrible shock when we were told she had Down's, we love her—and if we lost her now...' He didn't need to finish the sentence.

'It's a bit of a juggle,' Matthew said, as honest as ever. 'I would have preferred to wait a bit longer because she's so small and frail, but in her case she'll only be getting weaker.'

'So what happens now?' The poor man's face was nearly as pale and sweaty as his daughter's.

'We'll get her settled in a bed and give her some oxygen to ease her breathing. Once she's a little more able to cope, we'll need to do some tests.'

'What sort of tests?' Now it was the mother's turn to grow pale.

'There'll be several of them, and the information we get from them will tell us exactly what state her heart is in and where and how big the hole is between her right and left ventricles. Then we'll know exactly what we're up against and can plan accordingly.'

Matthew was able to stay on the ward until Alice had been propped up and was settled on an oxygen supply. She had been fidgety at first when they'd tried to position a nasal catheter, but she didn't really have the energy to fight.

'I'll sort out the paperwork for those tests. In the meantime, if you're worried about anything, just get Sister Morgan to give me a buzz.'

Hope's eyes followed his striding form as he made his way towards her office, then she sternly dragged her eyes back to concentrate on their newest little patient.

Alice was operated on a week later. Once it was obvious that she wasn't going to improve any further Matthew made the decision, although he was obviously far from happy with it.

'Her respiration is still much faster than I'd like, and even with frequent feeding she's still too frail, but that heart murmur is nearly loud enough to hear from the other side of the ward.'

'Would a few more days make any difference?' Hope was playing devil's advocate.

'There's the risk that she'll pick up another respiratory infection, and that would pull her all the way back down again. If that happens I'm pretty sure we'll lose her—she just hasn't got any reserves.'

'She's such a plucky little girl too. So even-tempered—even when we have to do all the tests.' Hope smiled pensively as their eyes met in accord.

'Hope. . .' When he turned towards her it was the first time in weeks that the expression on his face was not that of Mr Benedict, consultant paediatrician, but Matthew Benedict, the man she loved.

Hope couldn't bear the searing memory.

'No,' she whispered harshly. 'There's nothing to say.' And she whirled to leave her office.

'Jane phoned me,' he said over her objection, and she stopped as if she'd hit a brick wall.

'Is she all right?' The words were torn out of her. 'I haven't heard from her since she took the dresses back with her.' She wrapped her arms around herself for comfort and gripped her elbows as she slowly turned back towards him.

'She finished the hems,' he said. 'They went up to London to find the shoes they wanted. Look, Hope, we need to talk about—'

'No, Matthew.' There was such pleasure in saying his name, even though it was only to deny him. 'It's better this way in the long run.'

'For whom?' he demanded, the words harsh in the minimal privacy of a room with one glass wall and an open door. He threw his hands up in surrender and groaned in disgust. 'Have it your own way,' he muttered, and strode past her.

After he'd left Hope felt guilty for refusing to listen to him, and wished she could call him back again.

She knew that he was going straight to Theatre and wouldn't be coming back up to the ward before she came off duty, and she knew that she didn't have to worry that he wanted to talk to her about anything other than the wedding, but. . .he'd said he'd spoken to Jane, and Hope was starved of news of her daughter.

Hope tried phoning again that night, and for the first time in more than a month wasn't answered by a machine.

'Jane?' Surprise almost robbed her of her voice when her daughter answered.

'Mum?' The single word was cool.

'I—I just wanted to let you know that the cake is finished.' She sounded quite breathless.

'How has it turned out?' There was little enthusiasm in her tone.

'I'm. . .I'm pleased with it,' she said hesitantly. 'The sugarcraft flowers I've made for the top match the colours of your materials exactly.'

'Oh. Good.' Hope had the feeling that Jane was waiting for her to say something else, but she had no idea what.

'Edward's uncle told me you'd phoned him.' She was having difficulty dragging any more than monosyllables out of her, but she had to keep trying.

'And what did you think?' This time her words were an outright challenge, but Hope still didn't know why.

'Think? About what?'

'About the fact that I've asked him to take me up the aisle.'

Hope was shocked into silence.

'Well?' her daughter demanded. 'What did you say to him?'

'Nothing. . .' Hope's brain seemed to have

developed a short circuit. 'I mean, he didn't tell me, so I didn't know that—'

'You said he'd spoken to you.' It was almost an accusation.

'He told me you'd finished the hems. . .' In a minute this conversation was going to start making sense.

'If you weren't being so mean about my wedding he'd have told you what we decided. When we asked him to pay for the reception he was only too willing. Not like you. We knew you'd try to spoil everything for us. . .'

Her words faded as Hope suddenly realised how wrong she'd been about Matthew's involvement in the financial side of the wedding.

It was obvious now that he hadn't offered to go behind her back, but had been the innocent victim of a pair of scheming, selfish—

'Well—' Jane's strident tones broke through Hope's thoughts '—it doesn't really concern you, because it was my decision to ask him. I'm just glad that my gran isn't here to see how much I'm missing out on because of you.'

'What?' Hope was reeling. 'What are you talking about?'

'Oh, I've known about it for some time. Gran told me.'

'Told you about what?' The whole conversation was taking on a surreal slant, with every sentence confusing her more.

'That it's *your* fault that my dad isn't here to walk me up the aisle and give me away.' There was bitter venom behind the words.

'*What. . .?*' Hope felt sick.

'Gran said he committed suicide because you didn't love him enough.'

It was a good job that Hope was sitting down or she would have collapsed in a heap.

'You drove him to it.' Jane's voice continued to parrot the twisted lies that Hope had prayed her daughter would never hear. 'And then refused to let my gran help you look after me, so we've always had to scrimp and scrape, always had to have second best. Well, I wasn't going to have second best for *my* wedding. Why should I? It's my *right* to have a really super wedding if I want to. . .'

There was little Hope could say in the face of such a barrage of animosity, and she ended the call as soon as she could. She tried to tell Jane that she had her blessing to walk up the aisle with Matthew, but all she had received was a sharp reminder that as it was already arranged her approval didn't matter.

'Sometimes I wonder if *I* matter,' Hope murmured as she gazed blankly into the distance. 'How could I have been so blind about how nasty and grasping Jane was underneath all the sweet smiles?'

Of course, it didn't help that she'd been told so many lies by her grandmother. Hope hadn't wanted to blacken her daughter's ideas about her father, and had carefully only told her about their good days together in their childhood. If she'd been honest with Jane her grandmother wouldn't have been able to poison her mind, but Hope knew that it had been deliberate— her mother-in-law's revenge. . .

Now she had some serious thinking to do.

The first and most important thing was to speak to Matthew, to apologise for the hurtful things she'd said.

Hope could see now that it had been her own insecurities which had allowed Jane to wreak such havoc in her life. She had always felt guilty that Jane hadn't been able to have as much as other children but had believed that her unstinting love would be sufficient compensation.

Obviously it hadn't.

As Hope sat curled up in the corner of the settee cradling a large mug of tea she began to put a lot of things into perspective.

She realised that her daughter had been gradually pushing her into the background of her life for some time—almost as if she was ashamed of her. As if having a mother who went out to work, even though her job was something as worthwhile as nursing, was something to be hidden away.

Another thought slid evilly into her mind. Was there a deeper purpose in all Jane's confrontations with her over the wedding? Was she, perhaps, piling insult onto injury in the hope of causing such a rift with her mother that she wouldn't attend the wedding at all?

That would make sure that she wasn't embarrassed in front of her new friends by her unsophisticated mother.

Hope drew in a deep breath and released it before she uncurled herself and stood up.

First things first.

Tomorrow morning she was going to see Matthew as soon as she arrived at the hospital and ask to speak to him. She would explain exactly what Jane had been doing and how it had caused Hope to overreact.

In her heart of hearts she knew that there was very little chance that the two of them could resurrect the relationship she'd killed, but if he accepted her heartfelt apology perhaps they could at least be friends.

As far as the wedding was concerned, she would tell him her feelings about it and voice her reservations about attending. She had no wish to go where she wasn't wanted.

In spite of her efforts to control it, a cynical smile curled her mouth. If she was right in her suspicions, it was hardly a coincidence that her daughter had reserved her final outpouring of venom until she had heard that the cake was ready...

'Have you heard, Sister?' Mrs Harrison caught her as she was going past the end of the corridor leading to the intensive care unit on her way to her own ward. 'The operation went very well—I've just been across to tell them in Paediatrics.'

'I'm so pleased.' Hope smiled and gave her arm an encouraging squeeze. 'I'll keep my fingers crossed so that Alice can come back to my ward as soon as possible.'

'You just missed Mrs Harrison,' Ben told her as she arrived. 'Came down to give us an update on our Alice.'

'I bumped into her in the corridor and she told me.' Hope frowned. 'Poor woman looks as if she could do with a solid week's sleep just to catch up with herself.'

'There's more than one person around here who looks like that,' the tall charge nurse commented pointedly. 'If I thought you'd acquired those dark circles living the high life I'd give three cheers, but as far as I can see something's been eating you up from the inside for several months.'

Hope felt the colour rise in her cheeks as she avoided meeting his eyes.

'Thanks for caring,' she murmured.

'Anything I can help with?' he offered diffidently.

'No. It's...a family matter. Something I have to get through on my own. Thank goodness it won't be long now...' She sighed and shrugged. 'Has Mr Benedict been round recently?'

'He shot through earlier on and said he'd be back later. Do you need to contact him?'

'It'll wait,' Hope said dismissively, even though she longed to get the horrible job over and done with. 'Anything new since yesterday?'

'We've had one in for overnight observation after a fall, and a status asthmaticus sent up from Accident and Emergency. She's been on the nebuliser and has perked up nicely. Other than that, it looks as if it's going to be a thoroughly ordinary day, thank goodness.'

'Ordinary?' Hope scoffed. 'What on earth could be ordinary in a ward full of sick children?'

As if they'd heard what she said, there was a call from Admissions to confirm that there was a free bed in the paediatric ward.

'Simon Barker is seven and has had Perthes' disease confirmed. He needs to come in for bedrest, possibly with traction.'

Hope reviewed the arrangement of patients already in the ward and decided on a quick shuffle.

Young Simon would be with them for a long time, and it was important that he wasn't stuck in a corner where he couldn't participate in the life of the ward. Yet he mustn't be too close to heavy traffic routes so that his traction apparatus made him a danger to himself and to other people.

By the time the Barker family arrived, the flurry of

activity was over, and the other occupants of the ward were waiting to greet the new arrival.

'What's the matter with you?' David Monks called across, with all the bravado of his six years. 'You hurt your leg too?'

'My hip,' Simon corrected.

'What'd you do? I fell off the shed roof and broke my leg. They had to put metal in it.' The latter was said with pride as he indicated the contraption making his leg look like a spare part from a robot.

'I got a disease in my hip.' Simon began walking towards David's bed as they were comparing notes, and when his mother would have stopped him Hope shook her head, allowing the youngster to make his slightly uneven way across the ward.

'He'll be tied down soon enough,' she explained quietly, so that her voice didn't carry to the two lads. 'He might as well have a few minutes to make friends while we check the paperwork.'

She called across to the two youngsters to let Simon know where his parents were going, then led them through to her office.

'It can all be a bit frightening at first, especially if you haven't had to bring a child to hospital before, but we like to make the ward as informal as possible so that children can relax.'

'What about visiting hours?' Mrs Barker queried. 'Only, my husband works shifts and I've got a part-time job.'

'Within reason, you'll be able to visit him at any time—especially if he's going through a bad patch. Obviously, for the sake of the other patients, we have to restrict the numbers of visitors, but other than that you'll find it will all fit in.'

'How long will he be here?' her husband asked.

'You would probably do better to ask the paediatrician that, but according to the books, the first stage of treatment for Perthes'—'

'The bedrest?' Mrs Barker interjected.

'That's right.' Hope nodded. 'That can take anything from six to fifteen months to restore his mobility, depending on the severity of the case. After that he'll be in a cast to position the ball-joint at the top of his leg deep into the socket. As soon as the X-rays tell us that everything has grown back to normal he can start spending longer and longer out of the brace, until he doesn't need it any more.'

'It sounds as if he's going to be in here for years.' Mr Barker sounded horrified.

'Not at all.' Hope smiled reassuringly. 'As soon as he's progressed far enough we send him home—and let you continue with his treatment there.'

'He said the only good thing about having to come into hospital was that he wouldn't have to go to school,' his mother joked as she tried to put a brave face on it.

'In which case, I've got some very bad news for him. . .' Hope laughed and told them all about the hospital's provision for continuing Simon's education.

By this time the two of them were looking far more relaxed about the whole procedure, their worried glances towards their son through the observation window having gradually become more normal supervisory ones as they watched him working his way around the ward to talk to the other patients and their families.

'We'll take good care of him,' Hope promised. 'If you've got any problems or questions, you've only got to ask.'

'When will the specialist be coming round to see him?'

'He'll be seen every day and often several times a day by one or other of the paediatric team. Mr Benedict will be coming round in a little while because we told him you'd arrived, so we probably ought to do something about getting that young man into bed before he comes!'

It was another hour before Matthew appeared, looking very preoccupied.

He spent some time with the Barkers, and left them clearly satisfied with his visit.

'You made a good job of explaining the likely course of events to the parents.' He smiled tiredly. 'It makes a great deal of difference when it comes to parent compliance with a regimen when the child goes home.'

'It's not so long ago that we had that other little lad in here...'

'Richard Paige,' Matthew supplied from his inexhaustible memory.

'So I haven't had time to forget the swotting up I did at the time.'

Hope watched as he rubbed the palms of both hands over his face, and she thought again how tired he looked.

'Problems?' she questioned lightly.

'Unfortunately.' He pressed his lips tightly together and shook his head. 'Alice isn't doing very well.' He looked up at her and Hope could see the pain he was feeling.

'What's wrong? The operation?'

'That's the frustrating part about it,' he complained, looking as if he wanted to thump something. 'The operation went beautifully, but in spite of antibiotic cover her temperature's going up. It doesn't look very good.'

'Oh, Matthew.' Hope reached out her hand and laid it over his in a spontaneous gesture of support. 'She could still make it. . .'

'It's going to take a lot more than crossed fingers. . . more like miracles,' he said in a low voice, and placed his own hand over hers and pressed it between his own.

'Matthew. . .'

'Hope. . .'

They both stopped and laughed, then each offered the other the chance to go first.

'I need to speak to you.' Hope finally found the courage to speak the words aloud.

'Any particular reason?' He sounded slightly wary.

'I spoke to Jane last night,' she said simply.

'I'd suggest coming round to see you this evening, but I'm going to be on call—especially with Alice so poorly.'

'I could stay on after my shift ends and we could brave the canteen food?'

'We'd also be braving the hospital grapevine,' he pointed out. 'Since you told me about it I've been listening to it and it's amazing. You can sneeze at one end of an empty corridor and by the time you get to the other end someone will ask how your cold is!'

'All we have to do is let one of the nurses know about Jane and Edward's wedding, and that would take care of any personal slant to the gossip,' Hope suggested, careful to let him know that she wasn't expecting too much from the approaching meeting.

Matthew was silent, his calm gaze very intent as he watched the expressions crossing her face, and Hope felt a thrill of optimism. It might be just because he was tired, but it almost seemed as if the sharpness was gone from the anger between them.

Perhaps it *would* be possible for the two of them to be friends after all.

Four hours later, they had only just sat down with their trays of surprisingly appetising-looking salad when Matthew's pager went off.

'Dammit,' he muttered as he straightened up from the table and strode across to the telephone.

Within seconds he was back.

'It's Alice. I've got to go back up.' He hesitated a second, then asked, 'Will you come up with me? We can always replace these.' He gestured towards their salads.

Hope left her meal without a backward glance.

'What's happened to Alice?' she asked as they made for the nearest bank of lifts.

'Her temperature isn't coming down and her lungs are becoming congested. Now it looks like heart block.'

'Poor little scrap. Can you use a pacemaker to keep her going?'

'I don't know if it's feasible.' He sighed as he leant his head back against the wall of the lift. 'God, sometimes I hate my job.'

'Only because you want to save everyone,' Hope pointed out as she watched him agonise over what he would find when they reached Intensive Care. She longed to be able to comfort him, knowing just how hard it could be to do everything in your power to help a patient and to know it wasn't enough.

'Mr and Mrs Harrison.' He greeted the couple with a tired smile. 'I'm just going in to have another look at Alice.'

'We wanted to see you before you did,' Mr Harrison said, putting out one hand to stop Matthew going straight through to see his daughter.

'Mary and I have been talking to the staff while we've been here with Alice, and we've seen how hard you've all worked to look after her, even though she's a Down's baby.'

'That was never a consideration—' Matthew began in a heated tone, only to be interrupted again.

'We know that.' Mary Harrison smiled through her tears. 'But we don't want Alice to have to suffer unnecessarily.'

'What she means. . .' Her husband paused to clear the thickness from his throat. 'We trust you to decide when you've done enough. We love Alice, but we don't want our selfishness to put her through agony.'

'Thank you.' Matthew's voice was husky as he held out his hand to shake each of theirs. 'It means a great deal to know that you trust me to do what's best for your daughter.'

'I'll stay out here with Mr and Mrs Harrison while you examine Alice,' Hope volunteered, and smiled her reassurance at Matthew.

'It should have been such a happy day,' Mary Harrison sniffed, and her husband handed her his handkerchief. 'Alice survived the surgery and. . .' She glanced across at her husband then back at Hope with a trace of pink across her too-pale cheeks. 'We found out that we're expecting another baby.'

'That's not why we said what we did about Alice,' her husband added quickly.

'I understand.' Hope nodded. 'The two things exist completely separately.'

'We were thinking that Alice would have the chance to be a big sister before this baby overtook her... always supposing that this one isn't Down's too.'

'You aren't in the high-risk age band,' Hope reminded them, knowing that they would have had counselling after Alice was born, when they'd joined the Down's Babies Association. 'It would be very unusual for the two of you to have another affected child.'

'But it wouldn't matter.' Mary Harrison smiled through her tears. 'We already know that we can love them and that we can cope with the problems.'

'We've done it once, so we could do it again— willingly. We have no doubt that he or she would be every bit as loving as Alice—' He broke off as the door opened.

Matthew beckoned the two of them to follow him, and Hope knew just from the set of his shoulders that the news wasn't good.

'She was just too tiny and too frail,' he said to Hope as he sank back onto her settee, exhausted. 'It would have been awful for her to have had to keep trying...'

'Matthew.' Hope put her hand over his. 'It was for the best.'

He sighed deeply, sinking into the thick upholstery.

'In my head I know you're right, but...'

'But you hate to lose one...especially one as sweet as little Alice.'

'You've no idea how wonderful it is to know that you understand...' He turned his head towards hers and their eyes met for long, silent seconds.

'Sometimes my understanding is a bit slow on the uptake,' Hope admitted wryly. 'Especially where Jane is concerned.'

'You said she'd contacted you?'

'No, I managed to speak to her only after a month of getting her answering machine.'

'The little madam.' He sounded quite shocked. 'She sounds as if she needs telling a few home truths.'

'You don't know how close that comes to my own feelings,' Hope said pointedly. 'I told her I'd finished the cake.'

'I hope she thanked you.' His tone was ominous. 'You've spent endless hours on that cake and those dresses.'

'Well...she said "good", then told me she'd asked you to walk her up the aisle.'

'And?'

'And she told me it was all my fault that her own father wasn't here to escort her.'

'*Your* fault? How on earth did she work that one out?'

'Apparently, before she died, Jon's mother told her the "truth" about her father's death—that he committed suicide because I didn't love him enough.'

'How *did* he die?' Matthew's forehead was pleated in thought. 'I can't remember you telling me any details.'

'I've never spoken about it, for Jane's sake. I didn't want her to think badly of her father even though she'd never known him.'

'What *did* happen?'

'He did commit suicide, but it was because I was going to go to the police about him beating me. I was terrified that next time he might kill me...' She shuddered. 'It was probably the thought of his mother losing face with the neighbours if his homosexuality came out in court that drove him to it.'

'But why would his mother have said that to Jane? It was a complete lie.'

'Revenge.' Her reply was swift. 'I didn't realise until months later that Jon had made me pregnant, and I was desperate to finish my training so I'd be able to support the baby myself.' Determination was clear in her voice.

'Jon's mother offered to take care of Jane while I worked, and her help was a godsend. It wasn't until I wanted Jane back to live with me permanently that she tried to persuade the courts that I was an unfit mother so that she could have custody.'

'And because she lost, she bided her time and then stuck the knife in,' Matthew put in. 'Knowing you'd been careful not to shatter Jane's illusions about her father.'

'It wasn't Jane's illusions I wanted to attack when I found out that she'd been playing ends-against-the-middle with the two of us.' Hope's voice roughened. 'She deliberately lied to me so that I would think you were going behind my back, and then systematically insulted me and everything I'd tried to do for her.'

'Hope...'

'Matthew, I'm thinking of staying away from the wedding.' She finally dropped her bombshell.

'What?' His voice rose incredulously.

'She'd be happier if I wasn't there. I've made her the

dresses and the cake, as I promised, but she obviously doesn't think that I fit in with her new circle of friends.'

'If you don't go then I'm not going,' he said heatedly, his eyes dark with anger. 'I've never heard such rubbish. You've every right to be there—far more than half of the people they've invited.'

'But—'

'But nothing,' he interrupted. 'Apart from anything else, she'd never forgive you if you didn't turn up, because her friends would ask her why...and *you'd* always regret the fact that you hadn't gone.'

'Oh, Matthew. You're right, of course. Even so, I wouldn't regret it half as much as I regret being so awful to you these last weeks,' Hope admitted, gazing at him through tear-filled eyes. 'I've missed you so much.' Her voice had sunk to a whisper.

'Oh, Hope, I've missed you too,' he murmured as he wrapped his arms around her and held her tightly. 'It was your down-to-earth common sense that kept me from exploding as the two of them kept demanding more and more.'

'I'm so sorry it's all been such a nightmare. This isn't what a wedding should be like.' She drew in a shaky breath, and once again her lungs were filled with the musky smell that could only be Matthew.

'It's as much my fault as anyone's.' He scowled. 'I must have been stupid not to see that I was overcompensating for Edward's loss of his parents. By giving him whatever he wanted I wasn't being generous, I was turning him into everything I hate—a selfish, greedy—'

'Shh.' Hope put her hand over his mouth. 'He's young. He'll learn...life will make sure of it. Especially if you make sure he knows that he's on his own.'

Matthew grew suddenly thoughtful.

'You're right, as usual, and I've just thought of the perfect way to get the message across.'

'What?' Hope was intrigued by the wicked sparkle which had returned to his grey-green eyes. 'Are we *both* going to boycott the wedding?'

'Don't be naughty.' He tapped her nose with the tip of his finger. 'No. The two of us will go together to keep each other sane, and at the end of the reception we'll be able to wash our hands of the pair of them. They'll have had their ridiculously expensive wedding and when they get back from honeymoon they'll be left in no doubt that they've got to make their own way from now on.'

CHAPTER TEN

'Why?' Hope demanded as she looked out at the dirty grey sky. 'After days and days of beautiful sunny weather it has to rain. Today!'

'I know,' Matthew murmured soothingly, his thumbs massaging the tension out of her neck and shoulders. 'It's August and it's supposed to be sunny, but when did that ever make any difference in England?'

'Her dress will be ruined,' Hope wailed. 'It'll get all muddy around the hem.'

'So what? It's not as if she's going to be wearing it on a daily basis. It's only got to look good until the photographer's done his stuff.'

'Matthew! Your pragmatism isn't helping things.'

'What about a kiss?' He wrapped his arms around her as she sat in front of the mirror and planted a teasing series of kisses down the side of her neck. 'I'm beginning to think your idea of staying away from the wedding has its merits,' he growled as his hands came up to caress her breasts through the fine silk of her camisole.

'I'm just grateful that Jane decided that she and the bridesmaids were going to spend the night at the hotel where the reception's being held.' She tilted her head back to allow his lips to wander down her throat.

'Me too,' he murmured as he looked up to catch the drowsy expression in her eyes reflected in the mirror. Behind them they could see the wildly rumpled expanse of Hope's new double bed. 'I wouldn't have been happy about spending the night away from you.'

Hope chuckled. 'Jane was really puzzled when I didn't try to persuade them all to stay here for her last night as a single woman. She was obviously expecting me to be upset.'

'She'll learn.' Matthew's voice was dry as he straightened up and glanced at his watch. 'We ought to be leaving in about half an hour if we're going to deliver the cake to the hotel before we go to the church.'

'I'm nearly ready.' Hope picked up her lipstick. 'I would have been ready earlier if someone didn't keep eating all my lipstick off and rumpling my clothes so I have to press them again.' She glanced significantly over her shoulder at the state of the bed and threw him a mock scowl, then grinned broadly at his boyishly unrepentant swagger.

The church was dingy and bitterly cold as Hope waited for the organist to begin the music Jane had chosen for walking up the aisle. It was only the fact that Matthew would soon be with her that made the wait bearable.

She glanced over her shoulder and saw the group of people silhouetted in the dismal light by the open doors, and recognised his broad shoulders and long lean legs as he waited patiently for someone to fuss with Jane's dress, then the music began.

As soon as Jane's hand had been passed over to a waiting Edward, Matthew slipped quietly into the pew next to Hope.

'Hello,' she mouthed silently. 'OK?'

He smiled and nodded, and they both faced the front of the church to follow the time-honoured ritual.

'Why do wedding photographers make it seem as if they're filming a five-hour cinema epic?' Matthew whispered in Hope's ear as she shivered uncontrollably in the damp, chilly churchyard.

'Perhaps he thinks he is,' she murmured through chattering teeth, wishing she'd put her winter coat on over her silk suit. 'Watch the way he waves his hands about to direct people into position.'

'Either that, or he's an off-duty traffic policeman. . .'

Hope was sorely tempted to laugh aloud, especially when one of Jane's more pretentious college friends stood so close to Matthew that he stepped to the other side of Hope and linked his arm through hers.

'Good move.' Hope grinned up at him, giving his arm a squeeze when she saw the pink of embarrassment shading his elegant cheekbones.

'Well, she was going to be inside my suit with me if she got any closer. . .' There was the sudden flash of the camera, catching the two of them gazing at each other, and Hope had a feeling that when that photo was developed everyone would be able to see their love for each other.

Their silly banter continued in the car on the way to the reception, and it was the only thing which sustained Hope through the interminable wait while the bride and groom's friends were whisked away into a side-room for several large drinks.

'Shall I see if I can get you something?' Matthew asked solicitously.

'I daren't,' Hope murmured as she sank into an

uncomfortably stiff chair in the hotel corridor. 'I'm far too empty to put any alcohol into my system. I'd probably be sick.'

'Who arranged this stupid idea, anyway?' Matthew was growing angry. 'There's supposed to be a reception line, so that everyone is introduced as they arrive. Then we can all go and sit down in comfort.'

Hope did her best to calm him down, but he was just about to storm into the increasingly noisy side-room when people started spilling out towards them.

'Thank goodness for that.' He glanced down at his watch. 'They've kept us waiting out here for over an hour.' He held his hand out to Hope to lead her towards the reception line.

'Ma...tthew?' Hope suddenly couldn't feel her legs, and her voice sounded as if it was coming from a long way away. 'I don't feel very...' The blackness came up to meet her as the long wait took its toll.

'Head between your knees...' Matt was speaking, but it was difficult to hear what he was saying with his hand pressing on the back of her head. 'She'll feel better as soon as she's had something to eat—it's seven hours since breakfast now.'

Her wobbliness gave Matthew the ideal opportunity to switch the carefully positioned seating arrangements so that he was sitting next to her, and she was comforted to feel his hand steal across under the cover of the white damask tablecloth to slide his fingers between hers.

'Not long now,' he murmured, and winked surreptitiously.

The food they were served during the next hour wasn't a patch on the meals they'd shared at the Thatched Cottage or the Manor.

Because they'd been kept waiting so long the soup was cold, and the chicken had congealed in the dried-up rice for the second course.

By the time it came to the tiny portion of soggy cheesecake Hope couldn't wait to have a piece of the cake she'd made. At least she knew that *that* would taste perfect... She smiled secretively at Matthew, then glanced across at the now two-tiered wedding cake displayed in all its glory, and gloated at the fate of the third tier.

Matthew had been prevailed upon to make a speech, and had promised Hope that he would make it mercifully short.

As he stood up Hope was more interested in her appreciation of the cut of his suit. She knew only too well that most men had to rely on clever tailoring to do wonders for their less than perfect bodies. As far as Matthew was concerned, it was the broad shoulders and lean perfection of his body that made the suit look good.

'Ladies and gentlemen,' he began, his deep voice cutting effortlessly through the babble of slightly inebriated chatter. 'I'm not the father of either of these young people, but I've been asked to stand *in loco parentis* for both.

'I have promised that this won't be a long speech—we all know how utterly boring it is to hear about the supposedly clever things they said when they were three...'

There was a ripple of appreciative laughter.

'All I will say is that I hope they will be as happy as they deserve to be...'

The round of applause covered Hope's murmur as Matthew sat down again.

'*That* was a masterpiece of *double-entendre*. You're very wicked.'

'Unfortunately it will have gone over the heads of most of the people here. They'll only have heard what they wanted to.'

The best man's speech seemed as if it would go on forever.

Matthew had started casting worried glances at his watch and Hope was wondering what had happened to their careful arrangements when the words from the other end of the table caught their attention.

'Those of us who have got to know Jane over the last year know how lucky Edward is that she's beautiful and intelligent, but until today we hadn't realised how talented she is too, until we saw the beautiful wedding dress she designed and made for herself. . .'

Hope's gasp of shock was mercifully covered by the sound of applause, and it was only Matthew's consoling grip on her hand that prevented her from crying out in her betrayal and anger. Jane had even claimed the credit for *that*.

When one of the hotel staff tapped Matthew on the shoulder the shock nearly made him leap in the air, in spite of the fact that it was the signal they'd been waiting for.

'Mr Benedict?' she murmured discreetly. 'I've been asked to give you a message from the hospital. . .'

Matthew thanked her courteously and reached across behind Jane to tap Edward on the shoulder.

'That was a message from the hospital. Hope and I will have to leave now.'

'Oh, no. You can't!' Jane wailed. 'It's our wedding reception. . .'

'And I'm sure you'll enjoy it much more once we're out of the way,' Matthew said diplomatically as he leant forward to kiss her cheek. 'We'll see you both some time after you get back from your honeymoon.'

He grasped Hope's elbow possessively and hurried her out of the room.

By the time they reached the front door of the hotel they were almost running, and halfway to the car it became a race—the two of them laughing like children let out of school for a holiday.

'The receptionist saw us,' Hope said as soon as she'd caught her breath, just managing to do up her seat belt before he started the engine.

'She's probably terribly impressed by how keen and eager we doctors and nurses are to get back to our patients.'

'Why did the phone call come so late?'

'I don't know,' Matthew said darkly. 'I'll find out when we get back after the weekend.'

'Have we still got enough time to get there?'

'Plenty,' he confirmed as he glanced across at her, and his smile warmed her right through.

He reached out to capture her hand, and drew it up to his mouth to press a kiss into the centre of her palm before he settled it onto the warmth of his thigh. 'Have I told you lately that I love you, Mrs Benedict?'

'Do you think they'll ever forgive us?' Hope murmured as Matthew refilled her glass with champagne.

'What was that line? "Frankly, my dear, I don't give a damn."' He sprawled back against the sumptuous pile of pillows, gently pulling her with him, and they gazed out at the stunning view of starlit sky over historic buildings.

'Is it how you imagined it?' He gestured towards the world-famous outline of the Eiffel Tower silhouetted against the paler stone of the nearby buildings.

'Better,' she purred as she stroked one smooth leg over the roughness of the blond hair covering his more muscular one and marvelled at her new freedom. 'I never imagined that when I finally got to see it I would be lying about scantily clothed with my new husband.'

The warm August breeze was blowing the long, sheer curtains inwards, bringing with it the scent of the flowers from the surrounding formal gardens.

'Did I thank you for my flower?' Hope reached up to cradle Matthew's cheek in her hand as she remembered the moment when he'd handed her a single rose to carry up the aisle to their own wedding, just two days ago.

'You did.' He turned his head to press a kiss into her palm. 'But I don't mind if you thank me again. . .' He raised one eyebrow, the wicked gleam in his eye as much reminder as she needed of how that episode had ended.

'Do you want another piece of cake?' She gestured towards the beautifully decorated table the hotel had provided as a fit setting for the missing top tier of Jane's wedding cake. 'Did you see the way Jane glared at me when she saw her cake was only two layers?'

Her chuckle was infectious, and their shared laughter was a symbol that the hurts were beginning to heal.

'I was far more concerned that our diversion wasn't going to come in time for us to get to the airport,' Matthew grumbled. 'Shaunessy had better have a good excuse for putting us through all that agony, or I shan't invite him to our next wedding.'

'Next. . .?' Hope was aghast.

'Well, having waited so long, I enjoyed the first one so much that I think I'll make it a regular thing. Perhaps every year. . . No, every month if it means I get a cake like that.'

'You're welcome to the cake if I get a honeymoon like this every time I bake one.' Her face was suffused with happy laughter.

'Our wedding *was* much nicer,' Hope murmured as she snuggled back into the curve of his arm.

'Yes. You were quite right about the difference.' He reached out to deposit his empty glass on the polished wood of the bedside cabinet, then relieved Hope of hers. 'The hospital chapel was plain and functional, but having just our special friends there made it feel cosy and full of warmth and friendship.'

'And Tim Shaunessy was on time with the rings,' Hope pointed out, lifting her hand to admire the simple gold band beside the dainty sapphire and diamond engagement ring he'd insisted on buying her.

'Thank you for *my* ring.' His voice deepened as he held his hand up beside hers to display the matching plain gold band. 'I had no idea you knew I wanted one. . .' He shook his head.

'Ah! I got Tim to do some sleuthing for me, then slipped it to him before the ceremony,' Hope detailed triumphantly. 'And he and Maggie both brought cameras. . .'

'And managed to take photos without making it seem like a remake of *Ben Hur*. . .'

Hope had worn the Wedgwood-blue silk suit she'd

made with Jane and Edward's wedding in mind, and Matthew had worn one of his dark suits, but most of their guests had still been in their hospital uniforms as they'd managed to slip away to wish the couple well.

'Everyone wanted us to stop and chat to tell them how we'd managed to conduct a courtship right under their noses without the hospital grapevine getting hold of it!' Hope chuckled, then pillowed her head over his heart with a happy sigh.

'I meant it, Hope,' Matthew said quietly, tilting her chin up with one lean finger until their eyes met. 'I meant every one of those vows. . .' He leant down to brush a gentle kiss across her lips.

'Oh, Matthew. . .' Hope breathed. 'I'm glad you understand now what I meant about real marriages. They *should* be like this—a joining of the lives of two people who have come to know each other and love each other because of their strengths and in spite of their weaknesses. . .'

As she reached up to curve her hand round the back of his head to pull it back down towards her she caught the gleam of her rings, and her heart leapt at their beauty.

But they were only symbols. Like the single ivory rose Matthew had presented to her, and which now lay pressed between the pages of the family bible that was all she had left of her own parents. They were precious, but she didn't need such fragile reminders—not when she had Matthew's honesty and trust to rely on.

'What made you arrange this weekend away in Paris?' she murmured drowsily as the events of the day finally began to catch up with her. 'And this hotel! It must be one of the top ones in the whole of France.'

She remembered standing open-mouthed when they'd stepped out of the taxi and she'd seen for the first time the place where they'd be staying.

'Because you deserve it, Hope,' he said quietly. 'You give so much of yourself to others—your skill, your love, your money—and you never count the cost to yourself.'

The expression in his darkening eyes was fierce as he brought his lips to hers and continued.

'This is the first time in a lifetime of making sure that you know that there's nothing second best about you. You were well worth waiting for...' And suddenly Hope wasn't tired any more.

MILLS & BOON®

Medical Romance™

Books for enjoyment this month...

CRISIS FOR CASSANDRA	Abigail Gordon
PRESCRIPTION—ONE HUSBAND	Marion Lennox
WORTH WAITING FOR	Josie Metcalfe
DR RYDER AND SON	Gill Sanderson

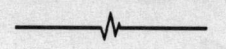

Treats in store!

Watch next month for these absorbing stories...

TRUSTING DR SCOTT	Mary Hawkins
PRESCRIPTION—ONE BRIDE	Marion Lennox
TAKING RISKS	Sharon Kendrick
PERFECT PRESCRIPTION	Carol Wood

Available from:
W.H. Smith, John Menzies, Volume One, Forbuoys, Martins,
Woolworths, Tesco, Asda, Safeway and other paperback stockists.

Readers in South Africa - write to:
IBS, Private Bag X3010, Randburg 2125.

MILLS & BOON®

Anne Mather
Collection

This summer Mills & Boon brings you a powerful collection of three passionate love stories from an outstanding author of romance:

Tidewater Seduction
Rich as Sin
Snowfire

576 pages of passion, drama and compelling story lines.

Available: August 1996

Available from WH Smith, John Menzies, Volume One, Forbuoys, Martins, Woolworths, Tesco, Asda, Safeway and other paperback stockists.

MILLS & BOON

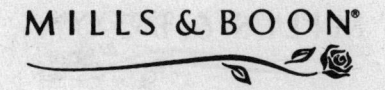

From Here To Paternity

Don't miss our great new series featuring fantastic men who eventually make fabulous fathers.

Some seek paternity, some have it thrust upon them—all will make it—whether they like it or not!

In September '96, look out for:

**Finn's Twins!
by Anne McAllister**

Available from WH Smith, John Menzies, Volume One, Forbuoys, Martins, Woolworths, Tesco, Asda, Safeway and other paperback stockists.

MILLS & BOON

Back by Popular Demand

BETTY NEELS

COLLECTOR'S EDITION

A collector's edition of favourite titles from one of the world's best-loved romance authors.

Mills & Boon are proud to bring back these sought after titles, now reissued in beautifully matching volumes and presented as one cherished collection.

Don't miss these unforgettable titles, coming next month:

Title #9   WISH WITH THE CANDLES
Title #10 BRITANNIA ALL AT SEA

Available wherever
Mills & Boon books are sold

Available from WH Smith, John Menzies, Forbuoys, Martins, Tesco, Asda, Safeway and other paperback stockists.

One to Another

A year's supply of Mills & Boon® novels— absolutely FREE!

Would you like to win a year's supply of heartwarming and passionate romances? Well, you can and they're FREE! Simply complete the missing word competition below and send it to us by 28th February 1997. The first 5 correct entries picked after the closing date will win a year's supply of Mills & Boon romance novels (six books every month—worth over £150). What could be easier?

PAPER	B A C K	WARDS
ARM		MAN
PAIN		ON
SHOE		TOP
FIRE		MAT
WAIST		HANGER
BED		BOX
BACK		AGE
RAIN		FALL
CHOPPING		ROOM

Please turn over for details of how to enter ☞

How to enter...

There are ten missing words in our grid overleaf. Each of the missing words must connect up with the words on either side to make a new word—e.g. PAPER-BACK-WARDS. As you find each one, write it in the space provided, we've done the first one for you!

When you have found all the words, don't forget to fill in your name and address in the space provided below and pop this page into an envelope (you don't even need a stamp) and post it today. Hurry—competition ends 28th February 1997.

**Mills & Boon® One to Another
FREEPOST
Croydon
Surrey
CR9 3WZ**

Are you a Reader Service Subscriber?   Yes ❑   No ❑

Ms/Mrs/Miss/Mr _____

Address _____

_____

_____ Postcode _____

One application per household.

You may be mailed with other offers from other reputable companies as a result of this application. If you would prefer not to receive such offers, please tick box. ❑

C496
A